Edwin Parker

The Hartford ordination

Letters of Rev. Drs. Hawes, Spring and Vermilye

Edwin Parker

The Hartford ordination
Letters of Rev. Drs. Hawes, Spring and Vermilye

ISBN/EAN: 9783337138066

Printed in Europe, USA, Canada, Australia, Japan

Cover: Foto ©Andreas Hilbeck / pixelio.de

More available books at **www.hansebooks.com**

The Hartford Ordination.

LETTERS

OF

Rev. Drs. Hawes, Spring, and Vermilye;

AND

Rev. Messrs. Childs & Parker:

REPUBLISHED FROM

The New York Observer,

WITH NOTES, AND A REVIEW:

TO WHICH IS ADDED

A STATEMENT OF THE MANCHESTER CASE.

—"For the Word of God, and for the testimony of Jesus Christ."—
Rev. 1 : 9.

HARTFORD, CONN.
ALEX'R CALHOUN & CO., PUBLISHERS.
1860.

PRELIMINARY REMARKS.

The publication of this pamphlet, though demanded, has been for some time delayed; and it would, perhaps, have been withheld altogether had not recent developments seemed clearly to call for it. It is no grateful task to review the acts of venerable men to whom we have been bound by many ties, but from whom we are now constrained solemnly and strongly to differ. No age, no relation, no reputation, can outweigh the claims of Divine truth. Nor are we wholly without hope that when the full force of these facts is fairly before our fathers and brethren, they may see and admit the peril which now threatens us.

Of the churches of New England we have the right to ask the earnest and candid attention. Their interests are most deeply concerned. It is easy to dismiss the whole subject with a smile, or a sneer, or with condemnation. Some will do so; but no intelligent, faithful and conscientious Christian. Those who regard the character of men more than the honor of the Lord Jesus Christ—who value the reputation of their pastors more than the truth of God—who place the *peace* of the church above its *purity*—will condemn this publication. But if any man who believes there is anything in the christian system worth contending for—anything in the faith of our Puritan fathers worth holding to—can read calmly the facts here established and not feel that there is cause for alarm, deep and sorrowful : if not for ourselves, for our children ; we have no more to say. It is, perhaps, due to the public that a fact should here be stated which, to every fair mind, will be an additional justification of the re-issue of these letters. Certain religious papers of considerable influence in New England have published article upon article on one side of the controversy, whilst studiously withholding from their readers the evidence upon the other side. How far this is just, manly or Christian, every honorable mind will judge for itself. In this pamphlet the statements of both sides will be found. If, therefore, any reader should differ from the conclusions of the reviewer, he has before him the material for his own judgment. For ourselves we have little to gain. Our heart's desire and prayer to God for our New England Zion is that she may be saved. If to this end this publication should be blessed, even in the least, we shall find abundant recompense and abundant consolation in all the obloquy it may incur. Whether we are right or wrong will soon be revealed ; but we beg to say, once for all, in behalf of ourselves and of our brethren in the faith throughout New England, to those who are wont to meet our convictions by ridicule and abuse, that these convictions are quite too deep and too solemn to be met by any such arguments. If we are wrong, this is not the way to convince us. If we are right, it is a vain and a thankless work thus to endeavor to silence us. In the fear of God, and of the tribunal where we and those who differ from us must soon meet, we submit these pages as our humble testimony " to the faith of God's elect."

The Ordination.

———— •‹•⟩•◦ ————

On the eleventh day of January 1860, Mr. Edwin Pond Parker was ordained and installed Pastor of the South Congregational Church of Hartford, Conn. Mr. Parker was a graduate of Bangor Theological Seminary; and had been recommended as "sound in theology" by the Rev. Dr. Pond, Professor in that Institution.*— The council by which he was installed was probably one of the ablest and most respectable that could be gathered in New England. It was composed of Pastors and Delegates from eleven Churches, and Professors from two Theological Seminaries. The examination was public, and in accordance with the invitation given, was attended by a large audience. Of course the facts which transpired were fairly public property. There could be no impropriety or reasonable ground of complaint in the use of those facts, provided they were of importance to the community.

A few weeks after the ordination the following letter appeared in the public prints. This letter was written by the Rev. Thos. S. Childs of Hartford, to a friend by whom it appears to have been sent to two or three papers for publication: §

---

* For the facts stated in this pamphlet, which do not appear in the letters of the Observer, we are indebted chiefly to the Independent; the Boston Recorder; the Congregationalist, and the Presbyterian Expositor.

§ Much has been made of this circulation of the letter; but it seems to us a very small matter. The question is, *are the statements true?* not, how far have they been spread?

THE LETTER.

My Dear Brother;—You ask me for some account of the examination of the young man who has just been installed over the South Church in Hartford. I give you the impression left on my mind, with a sad heart. This church, as you know, is one of the oldest, and has been regarded as one of the soundest in the State.

The examination was public; a large audience was present, and of course the views of the young man were no secret.

He rejected emphatically the verbal inspiration of the Scriptures. He was not clear on the Trinity, doubted as to the use of the word *Person*, and stated that the unity of God meant one personality.

All sin and holiness were affirmed by him to be voluntary.— God has no holy nature. Man has no sinful nature. Every man has ability (in the sense of "adequate power") to fulfil the commands of God, even to sinless perfection in the present life.

The gospel is not absolutely necessary to the salvation of adult heathen. Some are undoubtedly saved without it. God will give all men a fair chance, and Christ died with the same design for all. Hence if all men have not had a *fair chance* in this life, they will have it after death. The candidate stated openly, that he inclined to the belief that after death, and before the final judgment, there was a state (Hades) for all souls—where some who had died impenitent—some even who had rejected Christ in this life—would have a new offer of Christ and salvation, and the gift of the Holy Ghost, and be saved:—so that if called to the death-bed of an impenitent sinner, and knowing that he had but a short definite time to live, he would not shut him up to faith in Christ within that time, or final ruin.

These views were in direct conflict with the articles of the Church to which every private member is required to give his assent. Yet they were not regarded by the Council as a disqualification for the pastorship.

I hope that I am not a vain alarmist. Far be it from me to utter a word which should needlessly disturb the peace of our churches. But can any candid mind look at the events, so often now occurring, and not feel that there is a process going on, silently but surely, which by another generation must entirely change the character of our churches?

And one of the saddest things about it all is, that if any man is found to express anxiety about these things—if any man arises, who feels it to be a solemn duty to God to protest against the incoming errors, his reward is overwhelming ridicule as a man behind the age, or violent denunciation as a troubler of Israel.

Well—God is the judge. The day is coming which will reveal every man's work of what sort it is. My strong conviction is, that unless there shall soon be a mighty outpouring of the Holy Spirit, the day is not distant which will witness a more extensive and appalling apostasy in New England, than we have ever yet seen—and that apostasy will be into Universalism. May God in His infinite mercy avert the catastrophe.

Your Brother in the faith and work of Christ.　　　　C.

The New York Observer, in publishing the substance of this letter, said :—

"It is in harmony with what we hear from various quarters. The fact that a respectable number of ministers, in any part of our country, would consent to induct such a teacher as this candidate into the ministry, to preach such another gospel as the above, is enough to fill with painful apprehension the mind of every Christian who believes the truths there denied to be essential to the integrity of the gospel of Christ. * * * Apostasies are generally gradual. Scarcely any great defection in church history, however, has been so rapid as that which is now rushing to its crisis in New England.

To turn back the tide of corruption, to strengthen the things that remain, to save the rising generation from being borne away into the mire and misery of Pelagianism and Universalism, is a work that should command the active and untiring energies of every sound man in the church. Pastors should lift up no uncertain or trembling voice at such a time as this. The people, who love the faith of the noble fathers of New England, whose wholesome doctrines have been incorporated as the preserving salt in almost the whole body of sound churches in this country, the people ought to take the alarm, and by watchfulness, prayer and faithful labor, fortify themselves, their families and their neighbors against the inroads of this moral pestilence. Daily we behold the gathering evidence that a new reformation, the Reformation of the 19th century, must be preached and the Word of God, the doctrines of the cross, the faith of the Reformers and the Puritans, the system known as the EVANGELICAL, must be re-established in the heart of the people, to the expulsion of that rationalism, or semi-infidelity, that now threatens the ruin of the churches."

The publication of this letter produced a very marked impression both in and out of New England. On the one hand it was regarded as furnishing unexpected and alarming evidence of defection from fundamental truth; on the other it was violently denounced as slanderous or ridiculed as absurd.*

In the Observer of March 8th, Drs. Hawes and Spring appeared on the part of the council with the following letter which, with some variations, was also published in the Boston Recorder. §

---

* The *Independent* pronounced it a "calumnious article" whose author was to be "held to a strict account." The *Congregationalist* assailed it, its author and publishers, in an editorial surpassing anything we ever remember to have seen in its violation of all the courtesies of religious life.

§ Dr. Samuel Harris, Professor in the Bangor Seminary, also published an article in behalf of the council in the Recorder of March 1st. Dr. Spring appeared over his separate signature, in the Presbyterian Expositor of March 15th. Whatever is important to the case in these communications will be found in the notes.

For the New York Observer.

HARTFORD, March 2d, 1860.

Messrs. Editors:—You have noticed the examination of Rev. Mr. Parker, now pastor of the South Church in this city, which occurred on the 11th of January. *We*, the undersigned members of the Council, *request* you to publish the following article; and justice to the candidate in question, to the Council which ordained him, as well as the interests of religion in this city and state, demand this expression of our condemnation of the statements made in your issue of Feb. 23d, in regard to Mr. Parker. They who were present at the examination of the candidate, or know anything of it, need not be told, that your statements (or the statements you reproduced from an "intelligent" correspondent) were a succession of misrepresentations, exaggerations, suppressions and falsities. Your sources of information were strangely corrupt, and it is to be regretted that you should so unguardedly allow them to find an outlet through your columns. It is greatly to be deplored, that such careless, needless interruptions of fellowship are consummated. A misrepresented and maligned minister, a calumniated and aggrieved ministry, and an indignant Christian community—these are the results of a hastily published, or reproduced letter.

Your article, headed "New Gospel in New England," as a *whole*, is adapted to make only wrong impressions, and in *parts*, is utterly untrue. Mr. Parker read a somewhat long and particular creed before the Council, which was followed by a long and careful examination, chiefly in the line of the articles of faith adopted by the Church.

The creed referred to is before us, and this, with our own recollections, will enable us to state what is true in the case, and to correct what is untrue.

The first charge refers to "Inspiration." "He denied emphatically the verbal inspiration of the Scriptures." This implies that the candidate held such views as would invalidate the authority of Scripture. Hear his creed:

"The Scriptures of the Old and New Testament, * * * were written by men inspired of the Holy Ghost. They are a *unit*—a body, of which the various books are the members; each book has a polarity towards the cross of Christ; hence *all* this Scripture is inspired. It is the "Word of God." While the Logos is the Revealer and the Revelation, the Holy Ghost is the distinctive inspiring Power, enabling the sacred penmen to give an adequate expression of the truth, whether revealed to them, naturally apprehended by them, or simply communicated through them."

Whether this implies verbal inspiration or not, it contains all that is necessary to make the Scriptures a complete and authoritative rule of faith.

Only one gentleman proposed questions to the candidate on this topic. It was then nearly dark: the answers were very short, and thoroughly consistent with the article copied above. How unjust was the charge then!

The next statement is—"He was not clear on the Trinity: doubted as to the use of the word 'person.'" *Hear his creed:*

"I believe in God the Father, God the Son, and God the Holy Ghost. I believe in only one God. (Art. 1.) Christ is the God-human, the humiliation of the eternal Logos. The *proof* of this doctrine is found only in the Bible. It is a *rational* doctrine; and was chiefly held in the Apostolic and patriarchal church. I believe in the divinity of the Holy Ghost."

On being questioned as to his views of the Sabellian theory of one God manifesting himself under a three-fold name, he expressly discarded it as untrue, and admitted fully, as understood by the Council, the common orthodox views of the Trinity. He said the word "person" was often *misused* and misunderstood.

The third charge is—The candidate distinctly affirmed that "God has no holy nature, and man no sinful nature."

Yet he said in his creed, "God is essentially and eternally holy." Now the statement in your columns distinctly contradicts this, and is suited to make a false impression. The candidate did not choose to ring changes on the word "nature"; but regarding all holiness, and all sin, as predicable only of voluntary, choosing mind, he could not predicate holiness of the simple being or constitution of the Deity, nor sin of the passive, inert nature of man. But, lest we may not exactly represent him, let the candidate speak for himself:

"*Psychologically,* I believe holiness is the supreme choice of the mind, by which the person is devoted to the *universal,* rather than to his individual interests and good. I believe that *by nature,* men are sinners. That such is the corruption of the soul, that each person, obeying the influence of the depraved appetites and desires, will sin so soon as he comes to act consciously of the right and wrong. I do not believe that man is blameworthy, either for his nature or its hereditary corruption."

Who does believe so? or who can believe otherwise than this article expresses? The next thing charged is this—"The gospel is not absolutely necessary to the salvation of adult heathen." The candidate said no such thing. He explicitly stated, "there is *no salvation* without Christ!" He believed that some heathen, as some other persons who have never heard of Christ, may be renewed and saved through him, or on account of what he has done: but "*all by Christ!*" This is no new doctrine, nor is it any heresy. Watts, Emmons, Dwight, and other theologians held it, and it is taught in several confessions of faith adopted by the Reformed Church—the Presbyterian Church, and others.*

---

* Their letter in the Recorder contains the following in addition:—"As to what the letter charges, that the candidate holds that every man has ability in the sense of 'adequate power' to fulfill the commands of God"—let that speak for itself. It is accounted no deadly heresy, at least in this part of the country, to hold that man has power to do what God commands him to do; or, that he cannot be justly blamed or punished for not doing impossibilities."

The grossest charge of all is this:

"The candidate openly stated that he inclined to the belief, that after death and before the final judgment there was a state (Hades) for all souls where some who had died impenitent, and some who *had rejected Christ* in this life, would have a new offer of Christ, and the gift of the Holy Ghost, and be saved: so that if called to the death-bed of an impenitent sinner, and knowing that he had but a short time to live, he would not shut him up to faith in Christ within that time or to—final ruin."

Now there are several very sad charges made in this statement, not one of which was *held as an opinion* by the candidate. He explicitly stated, that though he sometimes inclined to the belief that the Bible spoke of an intermediate state or place of departed spirits, called Hades, still he was wholly undecided in the matter. He repeatedly stated, that for such as knew their duty and "*rejected* Christ in this life," he believed there was no future probation. This was his statement:—That for such as had never heard of Christ, had lived and died in ignorance of religious things, the *possibility* that there might be a future probation, sometimes entered his mind in the form of a *hope*, but never as yet as a settled conviction. He said that it floated in his mind as a thing that perchance might be, and claimed a place in his thoughts, not in his convictions. It was regretted by the council that his mind was in such an attitude in regard to this subject, but they could see in it no sufficient reason to refuse ordination.

As to the latter part of the allegation, "that if called to the death bed of an impenitent sinner," &c., it is enough to say that he explicitly stated that he should not feel influenced or authorized to broach the supposition of a future probation, either in public or in private, to an impenitent man. "Whatever my *secret hope* might be, I should hold out no such *unreliable* promises or hypothesis." It may be added that the candidate publicly signified his assent to such of the articles of faith adopted in the church of which he is now pastor, as were read to him. It is to be presumed he did it seriously and sincerely.

With that spirit of holy horror, which sees fanaticism in a manly frank way of stating the truth, we have no sympathy. It is said of the Roman army, that except the shedding of blood, a stranger could not distinguish their exercises from their battles. Did your correspondent, in his simplicity, mistake the animated discussions of that council in Hartford for veritable antagonisms? He is mistaken. Not a drop of blood was spilt, and candidate and council retired from the field on terms of tried fellowship. The wail of sorrow, which arises from your correspondent at the imagined apostasies of Connecticut churches, is so dolorously *soloistic*, as to sound very ludicrously about here! There is no foundation, save in a morbid imagination, for the lugubrious lamentations of said reporter.

The facts are now stated. How far they differ from those stated in the letter, the public must judge. No motives are imputed, no comments offered. No reflections are cast upon your correspondent. He must be left to his own reflections, which we can imagine must be not of the pleasantest character. We conclude with the earnest wish, that while he stands up manfully for the truth, he will not bring false accusations against his brethren; and that the next time he attends a council of Congregational ministers, assembled to ordain a Congregational pastor, he will *hear* with a more candid spirit, and report with a more accurate pen. *

J. HAWES,
SAMUEL SPRING.

---

*Dr. Spring, in his letter to the *Expositor*, says, that the impression made by Mr. Childs' letter is " totally at variance with the truth,"—that he " either stolidly misapprehended or wilfully misrepresented his (Mr. Parker's) views"—vouches for Mr. Parker's orthodoxy, and states that " the articles of faith adopted by the church of which he is now the pastor, were each and all openly accepted by him, not merely for substance of doctrine, but literally and in full." He notices only the one point of probation after death. He says, "The council were at first somewhat disturbed by it, but more particular investigation satisfied them that the suspected sentiment was not an opinion or belief adopted by the candidate, but only a floating thought, which he rather wished were true, than firmly believed. He did not " state openly that he inclined to the belief," that there would be a place and a mode of probation beyond this life, for any who had died impenitent; but that he had earnestly desired to hope, that in some peculiar, exceptional cases, where there had been no knowledge, and of course no rejection of Christ, there might be a probability that the mercy of God would provide a way by which the sin of ignorance might be pardoned, even beyond the grave. And when inquired of what was the foundation for such a hope, he stated that the passage in 1st Peter, 3 : 19, might possibly be regarded as furnishing some grounds for such an opinion. He said, however, explicitly, that for those who knowingly rejected Christ in this life, it was his firm belief that there was and could be no probation beyond that enjoyed, and such should be his uniform and unqualified teaching."

The following is the substance of Prof. Harris' defence.

"He (Mr. P.) rejected the verbal inspiration of the Scriptures," but distinctly affirmed his belief in the " plenary inspiration " of the whole Bible and of every part of it. He *was* " perfectly clear " in his statements on the Trinity, distinctly disclaiming the doctrine that the distinction of Father, Son and Holy Ghost, is one of manifestation only, and affirming that it is an *eternal* distinction in the Godhead, and that each of the Three is very God. He stated precisely and clearly the Orthodox doctrine. What he said of the term *persons* was the statement, familiar I had supposed to all theologians, that the term *person* is not applied to the distinctions in the Trinity in its full ordinary sense; that God is not one person in the same sense in which he is three persons. "He affirmed all sin and holiness to be voluntary," using the term *will* in the broader sense of Bellamy and Edwards, and not in the restricted sense which assigns to the will the function of volitions only. He affirmed that man's nature is corrupt, the occasion of the uniform certainty of sin from the beginning of moral action, but declined to predicate sin of the nature itself on the ground that a man is not accountable for a nature that is born in him. He affirmed distinctly that all men are sinners by nature. He made the usual distinction between natural and moral ability, and affirmed natural ability to obey the law. He defined natural ability to be " the possession of *faculties* adequate to obedience."

As to the salvation of the heathen, he distinctly and repeatedly affirmed that no human being can be saved except through the atonement of Christ and regeneration by the Holy Ghost. He expressed his belief, however, that some heathen have in

MR. CHILDS' REPLY.

For the New York Observer.

THE ORDINATION IN HARTFORD.

Messrs. Editors:—If the writer of the letter referred to in the Observer of Feb. 23d desired to awaken a spirit of theological inquiry in New England he seems likely to succeed. From Bangor to New Haven the depths are stirred. Out of this we fervently hope good may come.

In regard to the letter itself, allow me one or two remarks. It was written to a friend—a Congregational minister—in reply to a request for some account of the examination. The writer of the letter did not send it to any paper for publication. This is not said to avoid any just responsibility whatever. It is stated simply as a fact, and to meet certain statements from other quarters. As to the spirit of the letter we are quite willing to leave it to be compared with the replies.

Two replies have appeared; one in the Boston Recorder, understood, by an editorial note, to have been from Rev Dr. Harris, Professor in the Theological Seminary at Bangor, and father-in-law of the candidate; the other over the signatures of Drs. Hawes and Spring. It is with the latter that we now have to do. It is to be regretted that these gentlemen should so far have forgotten their position as to have indulged in such exhibitions of feeling.— Truth can afford to be calm. Hard words and hard names are no answer to facts.

A word to yourselves, Messrs Editors, to relieve somewhat the pain of the reflections these venerable fathers have cast upon you. We assure you that this "Christian community" is not all "indignant"—the Christian "ministry" does not feel itself "calumniated and aggrieved"—and whether the "minister" has been "misrepresented and maligned" is a point to be determined when the evidence is in.

---

this life been renewed by the Spirit without the knowledge of the Gospel, and so prepared to receive Christ whenever made known to them.   *   *   *

As to the intermediate state, instead of affirming that "some who had rejected Christ in this life would have a new offer of Christ and be saved," in the next, the candidate explicitly and repeatedly declared the contrary belief. But he said that in considering the case of the heathen and others who died *without hearing the Gospel*, he had in his perplexity sometimes conjectured that they might have an offer of mercy in the intermediate state; yet he repeatedly affirmed that this conjecture had never amounted to a *belief* that such an offer would be made, nor could he even say he *doubted* the commonly received doctrine; but only that it was a conjecture and a difficulty which had perplexed him and prevented his affirming without any qualification, his belief that there is absolutely no provision for the offer of mercy to persons of this class after death. He also stated repeatedly that he found no reliable evidence in the Bible justifying this conjecture; that the teaching of the Bible uniformly concentres on the duty of repentance and faith *now*, giving no intimation whatever of hope to any beyond the grave; that therefore, he should feel bound to preach according to this scriptural pattern."

We now come to the case in hand—the ordination of Mr. Parker. The question is this: "Were the position and views of Mr. Parker, *as explained by himself* on his examination, such as to justify his ordination and installation over an orthodox Congregational church of Connecticut?"

Drs. Hawes and Spring appeal to his creed. This is their main reliance. In regard to this we observe (1) That there are no men on earth who *ought* to know better than Drs. Hawes and Spring the utter insufficiency of a written creed to prove a man's soundness in the faith in New England. Do they need illustrations?

(2) If that creed was sufficient and decisive why the long and tedious examination that followed? What was the use of that oral examination at all, unless it was to reveal *in what way the candidate interpreted his creed?* With all due deference to these venerable men we beg leave to take the candidate's own interpretation of his creed rather than theirs. And this is precisely what was done by the writer of the letter. This is what we shall insist on doing. The reading of the creed excited no special attention —it was defective—it foreshadowed some of the subsequent developments; but it was not until the oral examination was fairly opened that the very serious errors and defects of the candidate's views were revealed.

(3) Subsequent events throw some light upon this point. If we are not misinformed, Mr. Parker's first sermon after his ordination was from the words, "By their fruits ye shall know them;" and unless he was grievously misunderstood by intelligent minds, the burden of that sermon was this—a man is not to be judged by his *creed* or his speculative faith, but by his life. As an illustration of his meaning he maintained that in his judgment the author of that fiction, "the Conflict of Ages," was just as good a man and just as reliable a religious teacher as if he had never held or published those speculations! Are Drs. Hawes and Spring ready to endorse this also?

Thus much for the force of a written creed.

In addition to the creed, these gentlemen rely upon their memory. Let us give this all due weight, remembering that it is called into exercise six weeks after the transactions occurred. The writer of the letter relied upon *written notes of the examination taken down at the time from the candidate's own mouth.*

There is one thing which will strike most minds as quite remarkable in the memory of these venerable men. They undertake to remember, after an interval of weeks, not only what *was* said, but what *not* said, through a tedious and at times, confused examination of three or four hours. And they undertake to remember exactly alike. The thing is simply a moral impossibility; and we shall have occasion to show that it fails as a matter of fact. These good men have quite overdone the matter at this point.

Now for the statements of the letter.

1. The candidate rejected the verbal inspiration of the Scriptures. This is admitted on all hands. Here, then, the letter stands justified. But the defendants appeal to the creed; and say that but "one gentleman proposed questions to the candidate on this topic." Here, at the outset, is an illustration of what we have just said as to the memory of the witnesses. They affirm positively and without the least hesitation, that "only one gentleman proposed questions to the candidate on this topic." There were at least two, who examined him at different times. Now when the memory of the witnesses "agreeing together" fails upon so palpable a point as this—the asking and answering, not of a single question, but of a series of questions—we submit whether it does not throw a doubt upon their equally positive assertions on other points.

They, however, fix the *time* of this examination, and this indicates the gentleman to whom they refer.

Now what is the evidence of that gentleman? He affirms, and is ready to affirm, if need be, under oath, the substantial truth of the following statement: To the question, "Do you believe in the plenary inspiration of the Scriptures?" the candidate declined to give a direct answer, but replied that he did not know that he exactly understood what was meant by plenary inspiration. To the question, "Are you prepared to admit verbal inspiration?" he replied, with an emphasis more significant even than the words, "I am prepared to *reject* it!"

Now this is a case directly in point in regard to the creed. The venerable gentlemen tell us to "hear his creed." We do hear it; it sounds pretty well; we hear him say that "all this scripture is inspired." But we want to know what he means by inspiration; we have heard in these days of other writings being inspired—we want to know what *Mr. Parker* means by inspiration; he says it is such an influence as enables the penman to "give an *adequate* expression of the truth"—we are troublesome we know, but we want to understand again what he *means* by an "adequate expression of truth." We presume that Drs. Hawes and Spring think they have given an "adequate expression of the truth" in their rejoinder; but we do not think it is inspired; so we ask the candidate in the plain old language of the Church and of the Evangelical faith, if he believes in *plenary* inspiration; and he does not know what it means; and we ask him if he believes in *verbal* inspiration; and *then* we have an answer.

We must say, however, that we were not surprised that the Council were not disturbed by the candidate's views of inspiration; we were prepared for this by previous experience. We had seen a man examined and ordained, by a council composed in part of the same men, who stated openly that there were parts of the Bible which were not inspired—that the Holy Spirit suffered them to remain because He saw they wouldn't do any hurt—and we had heard the venerable Dr. Hawes express the highest satisfaction at the examination of that gentleman. From that time forth we have ceased to be surprised at any errors to which this venerable man may have given his sanction.

2. As to the Trinity. The letter says *he was not clear;* he doubted as to the use of the word person; and stated that the unity of God meant one personality. The last two statements are exegetical of the first. We will go back from these to that. Now for the proof. To the question by Dr. Spring, "What do you mean by the unity of God?" the candidate answered with some hesitation, but in these very words, "I mean *one personality.*" This point the venerable gentlemen who undertake to "state what is true and to correct what is untrue," do not touch.

"He doubted as to the use of the word *Person,*" says the letter. "Hear his creed," cry the defendants. We do hear it, gentlemen, but we do not hear in it the first letter of the word "Person." What is the meaning of this? Will you tell us, if the candidate *was* clear on the Trinity, why, in a deliberately written article upon this great subject, he utterly ignores the tri-personality of the Godhead!

The Confession of Faith of the Congregational churches of Connecticut says: "In the unity of the Godhead there be *three persons* of one substance, power, and eternity," and it declares the "doctrine of the Trinity to be the foundation of all our communion with God, and comfortable dependence upon him." We would reverently but earnestly suggest to these venerable fathers of the Church to beware what countenance they give to the undermining of this great doctrine.

The explanation which Dr. Harris gives of the candidate's position upon this subject, which position he affirms to be "perfectly clear," is striking and to us original. He thinks that all the young man meant to say was, "that God is not one person in the same sense in which he is three persons;" a statement which he supposes familiar to all theologians. Now we are not a professor of theology as Dr. Harris is; but this statement which he supposes "familiar to all theologians" is entirely new to us. We are quite familiar with the expression: "God is not *one* in the same sense in which he is *three;*" but that "he is not one person in the same sense in which he is three persons," is a fact which we do not remember to have ever before seen affirmed or denied.

We might safely leave this point of clearness on the Trinity here. There was an incident, however, in the examination, quite too much in point to be passed over. The candidate had read his creed upon the subject—he had been examined and cross-examined at length upon it—the work was nearly through. Dr. Hawes rose and said: "*All that you have said, sir, could be said by a Sabellian*—do you receive that doctrine?" The reply of the candidate was equally remarkable. "I do not know as I understand what Sabellianism is. I have tried to find out, but I have not been successful."

Now whatever answers may have been given to *leading questions*, to break the full force of this development, we submit that the case is made out. The candidate was not clear on the Trinity.

3. The statements of the letter in regard to sin and holiness, the nature and power of man, are really admitted by all the responddents. At a future time, if the way be open, we hope to take up their own statements and show how utterly opposed they are to the faith of Evangelical Christendom, to the Confession of Faith of the Connecticut churches, and to the Word of God.

We content ourselves now with giving, on the strength of our notes and the evidence of the Examiner, the substance of the candidate's statements on these points. He did distinctly affirm that there was no such thing as a sinful or holy nature. Man was sinful *through* nature, not naturally sinful. But who does not see the door of boundless errors opened here? Who does not see that this statement is perfectly consistent with the affirmation that man is born innocent and sinless? Did not Adam become sinful *through* nature? Did not the fallen angels become sinful *through* nature, or "*by* nature?" •

The gentlemen who have undertaken this defence would leave the impression, we presume, that Mr. Parker holds the honest old doctrine of *original sin.* And the members of the South Church in Hartford have no doubt read with great delight the expressions of his creed "by nature," "corruption of the soul," "depraved appetite," "hereditary corruption," &c.

Now we have one simple question to ask, and if these venerable gentlemen will answer it, it will be more to the point than a volume of explanations. Is that "corruption of the soul," that "hereditary corruption," *sinful* in Mr. Parker's view?

4. To a question by Dr. Spring, the candidate replied "that God did not require of man what he had no ability to perform." To the question in another form he said he should answer differently, according to the use of the word ability. (Q.) "Take the word ability in its proper sense of 'adequate power,' do you hold that man has ability in this sense to meet the requirements of God?" (A.) "I do."

(Q.) "Are you prepared to carry out that position to its logical results, and hold that man has ability to obey God perfectly in the present life?" (A.) "Yes, sir."

5. Another charge of the letter is, "the gospel is not absolutely necessary to the salvation of adult heathen. Some are undoubtedly saved without it." The candidate not only declared this in general, but he made a specific application of it: "I have no doubt,"

said he, "that Socrates went to heaven." The statement, whether true or false, important or unimportant, is undeniable.

6. The letter stated as a doctrine held by the candidate that "Christ died with the same *design* for all men." He not only stated this in general, but he affirmed in particular that "Christ died with the same design for Judas Iscariot as for the Apostle Paul." This the gentlemen do not deny.

7. We now come to the "crisis"*—Mr. Parker's views of the future state. And we shall meet the whole matter by a simple statement of facts which we stand ready to verify before any tribunal.

(1.) The germ of his views was *in his written creed*. Why did not Drs. Hawes and Spring ask us to "hear his creed" on this point?

(2.) After an examination upon the subject which had gone on to weariness, with questions and cross questions, with explanations and counter explanations, the candidate did say frankly and explicitly, "I wish to conceal nothing; *I will state my position upon this whole subject*. I INCLINE TO THE BELIEF that there is after death a state (Hades) for all souls, good and bad, where the good are happy, and where some who have died impenitent, may have a chance of salvation," &c. In reply to inquiries he stated that he supposed this salvation would be in connection with the means of grace—the offer of Christ and the gift of the Holy Ghost.

(3.)—He not only stated it; he argued it; feebly and doubtfully indeed, but he argued it. He said he thought there were passages of Scripture which pointed to such a state, e. g., "Christ preached to the spirits in prison."

(4.) He not only argued it, he called upon the Council to prove that the doctrine was not true. "Will any one quote to me a scriptural proof against this view?"

(5.) When asked to reconcile his doctrine with the articles of the church over which he was about to be installed, and which articles affirm that men are to be judged "according to the deeds done in the body," he replied that he should not interpret the "deeds done in the body," as referring strictly to the present life.

(6.) He applied his theory, not merely to some who "had never heard of Christ," but to those who had heard and died unbelieving. Surely the gentlemen cannot have forgotten the case so solemnly put and so unequivocally answered: "Suppose, sir, you were called to the death bed of an impenitent man, and knew that he had but ten minutes to live; would you tell him that he must repent and believe in Christ within that time or be lost?"

---

* This was the word used by Mr. Parker in his creed, to denote that point of time beyond the grave, up to which he was understood as entertaining hope for some who died impenitent.

(A.) " I would not!" Nor can they have forgotten the earnest exclamation which burst from the lips of the venerable Dr. Hawes, " *Then he would never repent!* "

It is true the candidate did say that his doctrine was " not *expressly* taught in Scripture "—it is true he admitted that the general drift of the Bible shuts men up to the present; but this only makes the matter worse, and is a most significant comment upon his views of inspiration. In the most solemn moments of his ministerial life—in the very article of death—standing to usher an immortal soul through the awful portals of eternity, *he declares that he will not shut that soul up, for its everlasting hopes, to the point of time to which he admits the whole burden of God's word shuts him up!*

Gentlemen of the Council; is there here no practical issue of the faith you have ordained? Does it not pierce to the very heart of the glorious gospel of the blessed God? It is *not* " enough "—it is solemn trifling for you to tell us that there was *something else* also, which he said he would not do. There was *this* which he said he would not do, and this which takes hold upon the whole matter of the eternal destiny of men.

The denial of Drs. Hawes and Spring here amounts simply to this—that Mr. Parker, when called to the death bed of a sinner, would not deliberately sit down and comfort him with the hope of a future probation. If this is " enough " for these worthy men, we are very sure it is not enough for the Christian community. Nor is it the question;—it is not whether Mr. P. would positively preach a future probation, but whether he would positively preach *Christ received now* as the sinner's only hope! He declared that he would not. Whether this be, as the *Observer* says, " another gospel " or not, let the world judge. It is not the gospel we preach; it is not the gospel Christ preached.

And yet these gentlemen did not hesitate to present a man in this state of mind as a qualified guide and teacher of a flock of Christ! We recall that. If the reports are true, which from various quarters are now floating through the community, that secret session of the Council was not as harmonious, nor the final vote as unanimous, as the statements of Drs. Hawes and Spring would seem to imply. If there be any foundation for these reports, gentlemen, you *did* hesitate, you doubted, you feared. You listened to earnest explanations and fervent appeals from the theological instructor and near friend of the candidate—you hoped, and you yielded.

Drs. Hawes and Spring have been pleased to charge the author of the " Letter " with a succession of misrepresentations, exaggerations, suppressions, and falsities. They have been pleased to state that all " who were present at the examination, or knew anything of it," understand this to be so.

Now we call upon them to throw open the doors of that secret session, and let us know the impression made by the examination upon the minds of the fathers and brethren there. Tell us if it be true that votes were obtained for the candidate, not on the strength of his examination, but in spite of that examination, and on the ground, simply and solely, of the explanations, apologies and appeals of his theological instructor and friend! Tell us if you had a divided vote at last, and give us the names of the men who refused to go with you in your final deed! Let us summon them— and we do summon them, wherever they are—to give their testimony in this case. The cause of truth demands it. *Give us, gentlemen, the whole and faithful history of that secret Council;* and we consent to leave the case to the decision of the public!

A word more and we yield the pen. We give place to no man in all due respect for the age, position, and reputation of the men whose statements we have felt called upon to review. But the truth of Christ is more sacred than the person of any man. In our inmost soul we believed that that truth was imperilled—we believe so still; and though every member of the Council should sign the letter of Drs. Hawes and Spring—which they never will —we appeal the case to coming time and a higher tribunal.

You have, Messrs. Editors, my name, which you are at liberty to give, whenever it shall be essential to the cause of   TRUTH.

Hartford, March 12, 1860.

In some editorial remarks connected with the above letter the *Observer* stated that the Rev. Dr. Vermilye, Professor of Theology in the Seminary at East Windsor, Ct., was on the Council ; and called for his statement. Dr. Vermilye responded in the Observer of March 29th—

STATEMENT OF REV. DR. VERMILYE.

Messrs. Editors :—As my name has been mentioned in the Observer, and elsewhere, in connection with the recent ordination at Hartford, it seems due to truth, that I should explain my position in that case. As you intimate, I was a member of the ordaining council, and on the examination of the candidate was constrained to cast my vote in the negative. I differed with great reluctance from venerable and respected brethren : but my judgment and conscience permitted me to take no other ground, than that of opposition to the ordination, under the circumstances. And subsequent reflection has not led me to doubt of the propriety and necessity of my vote.

In regard to the discussion to which the ordination has given rise, perhaps the foregoing statement may be sufficient to indicate my view of the facts. It is hardly necessary to say, that they appeared to me, *in all essential particulars, as your correspondent represents them.* I will, however, add that I have read his last communication with some care, and am prepared to affirm its substantial truth. There are two or three of his statements which I cannot distinctly confirm, as my attention was partially diverted during that part of the questioning. Their truth however, with a single exception, is conceded, I believe, by the other writers: while similar though not identical answers were given by the candidate at other times. As it respects the last point, that of probation after death, —(which it may be said occupied more than half the time of the examination,) according to my recollection, *his statements are entirely accurate.* In my judgment they leave a fair and just *impression* of the candidate's views, as defined by himself before the Council. And if the anxiety manifested by more than one member during the public examination, is any index, it is the impression which they were naturally calculated to give. It was exceedingly painful to me to reach the conclusion, that such were his views ; but I did not see how to avoid it.

At present I limit myself to these brief statements. But if circumstances should demand it hereafter, I shall be prepared to state more fully my reasons for the vote I was constrained to give.

ROBERT G. VERMILYE.

East Windsor Hill, Ct., March 23d.

April 5th, Drs. Spring and Hawes replied to Mr. Childs.

For the New York Observer.

REV. DRS. SPRING AND HAWES REJOINDER TO REV. MR. CHILDS.

Messrs. Editors :—We are constrained to ask, once more, for the indulgence of your columns, and for the last time on this subject, that we may disabuse if possible, your own minds, and those of your numerous readers, of the errors which might very naturally be imbibed from an implicit reception of the article in your issue of 22d. inst., headed, "THE RECENT ORDINATION IN HARTFORD." We know not from what sources your correspondent has gathered his impressions of the manner in which his attack upon the Council and the candidate is received. We can assure him that, with very few exceptions, both his spirit and his statements meet with general and unqualified disapprobation. It would not be surprising if those who are eagerly watching for symptoms of heresy in the New England churches and their ministry, should hail with pleasure the assistance of a respectable ally ; but he may believe us when we say, that this sort of approval will afford him but little comfort when he comes to learn that his course in this matter is widely looked upon as an unaccountable expression of perverse and determined suspicion.

Your correspondent, in speaking of our letter is pleased to say, "It is to be regretted that these gentlemen should so far have forgotten their position as to have indulged in such exhibitions of feeling." We are not aware that we gave utterance to anything unbecoming in that communication. If anything in it has offended him, it may be well for him to inquire whether it was not imperatively demanded by his unprovoked assault, simultaneously made, in at least three different papers, and in parts of the land quite distant from each other.* This studied contiguity, in point of time, of the several and yet almost exactly similar blasts of the note of alarm, could not but awaken some surprise, and lead us to enquire if we were not, in common with our brethren of the Council, called upon to offer some defence. The occasion certainly would not justify rudeness, but it did call for a tone of distinct and well defined complaint. Is it then to be wondered at that some displeasure should be expressed at the fact that an anonymous attack was made upon the character, and regard for the truth, of a large Council, and upon the standing of a young pastor just introduced by us into the ministry, and henceforth to take part with us in the promulgation and defence of the gospel. If warmth were excusable in the discussion of such grave matters as your correspondent presented in his communication, it certainly might be pardoned in us, when we were thus unkindly arraigned, and charged with such delinquency to our Master's cause.

There is one point, though not a very material one, on which we are willing to defer to our brother's alleged confidence in his better means of information. We mean his statement that there were two, if not more, questions, or series of questions, put to the candidate on the subject of his belief in Inspiration; while our letter says that only one of the Council questioned him on this article.— We were not careful to keep an account of the number of examiners, nor even who they were. We felt that the main object of the examination was sufficient to absorb our attention, and made our statement on the authority of Mr. Parker, with respect to *this* part of it. He still says that we were correct in saying that only one took the lead in questioning him on this topic, and that if there were more inquiries, they were but interposed and occasional, and were no serious interruption to the general drift. However, it is easily seen that this is an unimportant point. Whether one, or two, or six questioned the candidate, is not so important as to learn what his views were. If our statement in this minute particular be incorrect, to the full extent even stated by your correspondent, let

---

*This is hardly candid, after the assurance that Mr. Childs had *not* made an "unprovoked assault in three different papers."

the error have its due weight. We do not peremptorily deny that it might have been a mistake; but if it were, we think it should not have been made the basis of a grave charge against our veracity, and insisted upon as invalidating our testimony in other particulars.[*]

Your correspondent has dwelt at some length upon what he regards as discrepancies between Mr. Parker's creed and his subsequent "interpretation" of it. We are gratified to learn that, in the opinion of your correspondent, the creed "sounds pretty well."[†] We think more than this; it sounds *very* well; and if the candidate could—and we believe he could—*ex animo*, adopt that creed, we did not feel, nor do we now feel, that his correctness in the faith should be called in question.[§] His subsequent examination, or if you please so to call it, his interpretation of his creed, was not an absolute necessity, but was entered upon in compliance with an honored and a general custom, partly to afford the candidate in such cases a more full opportunity to explain his views, and to satisfy any listeners, whether prejudiced in his favor, or possibly captious, that he is to be relied on as a firm friend, and able defender of the truth.

---

[*] If Drs. H. & S. will refer to Mr. Childs' letter they will see that he did not make "a grave charge against their veracity." They had not been as careful in regard to him. On points where it is now admitted that he was correct, they charged him with "a succession of misrepresentations, exaggerations, suppressions and falsities;" again and again they accuse him of falsehood; they sneer at his "intelligence;" speak of him as "a corrupt source of information," as having "stolidly misapprehended or wilfully misrepresented" the facts. Yet they see nothing "unbecoming" in all this. Mr. Childs had carefully forborne to retort their language. Even where it was perfectly evident that they were wrong, he ascribed their error to their memory. It now seems to have been a more serious thing than this. These gentlemen put forth positive statements, for the correctness of which they pledged the accuracy of their own memories. They now admit that upon this point they did *not* remember, but relied upon Mr. Parker for the fact. The "point," indeed, is "not a very material one," but it is material, as a matter of evidence, to know how many more of their statements were made on the same authority.

It is now no secret that these venerable gentlemen are willing to avoid the odium of their first letter, on the ground that *it was altered after leaving their hands.* This can hardly avail. To most minds it would be a very serious question, what moral right they had, in so grave a case, to allow a letter go out of their hands for revision and alteration. If they gave their names to Mr. P. or any other man, to be used at discretion, it is not they, but the public, who have the right to remonstrate at this further remarkable development in a very remarkable defence. It will be observed, moreover, that in their second letter, they fully endorse and defend the manner and spirit of the first.

[†] If these gentlemen will turn to Mr. C's letter, they will see that they have again misapprehended it. His remark was made in reference to a particular article. In regard to the creed as a whole, he said expressly "it was defective, &c." See p. 13.

[§] Why then did these gentlemen at one time "call in question the correctness of the faith" of Dr. Bushnell, who was willing to accept as many creeds as could be presented to him? On the ground on which they now stand, we do not see by what right they ever accused Dr. B. of heresy. Is it not possible that some ministers in New England have obtained a general reputation for orthodoxy, on the ground of their opposition to Dr. Bushnell on certain points, who, on other points, are even farther from the evangelical faith than Dr. B. himself!

And in this place, if at all, we might enter again into the particular items of Mr. Parker's belief, as set forth severally, and at length, in the article on which we are commenting. But after the full treatment of the matter in our former letter, and the endorsement of the pastor elect by the whole Council, with a solitary and greatly esteemed exception, this is the less necessary. We content ourselves, therefore, with a few general remarks, rather as supplementary to our former communication, than as a new and independent discussion.

On the subject of the verbal inspiration of the Scriptures; the use of the word Person in the statement of the doctrine of the Trinity; a sinful and holy nature in distinction from sinful and holy action; and moral and natural ability; it is perfectly well known that differences of opinion exist, not only between Presbyterian and Congregational divines, but between the advocates on the one hand, and the opposers on the other, of some forms of these doctrines, in Congregational churches reputed orthodox. Nay, if we mistake not, the Presbyterian Church is divided on some, if not all, of these topics. Your correspondent has seen Mr. Parker's views from his Presbyterian stand-point; and we have looked at them from ours. We hope we love the truth, and are resolute to defend it; but we have yet to learn that firmness in this position requires us to. "make a man an offender for a word," or would justify us in separating from those whom we love to claim as our natural allies in the holy cause of truth and God.

To the very disrespectful and unkind remark, that your correspondent has "ceased to be surprised at any errors to which (Dr. Hawes) may have given his sanction," the writer of this paragraph may be permitted to say that he marvels at its temerity. Dr. Hawes is too well known, here and elsewhere, to be seriously injured by such an insinuation. Why the pastor of the Presbyterian church in Hartford should have seen fit to go thus out of his way, and call up an isolated and detached circumstance connected with another installation, and admitting of full explanation, were all the circumstances known, is not easily accounted for. It reveals a spirit more bitter and unlovely than we had expected to witness in our Brother Childs. The topic is dismissed, however, with the comforting reflection that Dr. Hawes is fully competent to sustain himself, and stands in no need of the writer's feeble hand to repel any such accusation from any quarter whatever.

Allow us, Messrs. Editors, one word, in closing, with regard to the source from which you very honorably acknowledge that you received your communication. The author occupies a position, which, in our view, is not the best adapted to enable him to judge with fairness, or even report with impartiality, the entire character of the examination, of which he has given you a distorted and unfair account.

He is the pastor of a Presbyterian church, in the neighborhood of Congregational churches, whose defects, if there be any, he is interested to discover, and when discerned or imagined, under strong temptations to magnify and proclaim. Possibly this fact may have had too much to do with the *animus* of his communication—quite too visible for his reputation as a Christian minister and a candid observer. Your correspondent has been admitted, with all kindness, and without the suspicion that he would make any other than a friendly and honorable use of the confidence thus reposed in him, to the most unreserved disclosures which his brethren, of three denominations in the city, have made of their views of theological subjects. And no one knows better than he, that, on many points, their opinions are not in perfect harmony. Nor should it have appeared strange to him that in a large Council, composed of the pastors and delegates of eleven churches, all were not alike satisfied with the candidate's explanation of his creed. If in the main they were prepared to pronounce him sound in the faith, and as such could commend him to the confidence of the churches, this was all they were called upon to do in the circumstances of the case.

To the demand that the retired, and necessarily exclusive deliberations of the Council should be made public, we have only to say that it is a very unusual one. When was it known that a body selected for the express purpose of settling a question referred to their sole decision, should either call in to their aid the deliberations of others, in making up their result, or openly proclaim the possibility of minuter shades of differing opinions in their own body?*

And now, Messrs. Editors, we are happy to say that we have done with your correspondent, and we hope never to be unfortunate enough to meet with another so disingenuous and uncourteous. It is refreshing to turn to your own calm, dignified, and temperate statement of the whole question. It lies in a nut-shell. You are willing, and we honor you for the liberality, to put aside for the

---

* Here again Drs. H. and S. seem to have misapprehended the point of Mr. C's letter. They had denied the truth of his report, and had said that "those who were present at the examination or knew anything of it, need not be told that his statements were a succession of misrepresentations," &c. They had said (Bost. Rec.) that he was probably the only man who had received such an impression. They had represented the action of the Council as harmonious, and had left the impression strongly that on the whole it was a clear and satisfactory case to the entire Council; and had severely rebuked the papers that had given currency to any opposite impressions. Now the case was very easily settled. The Council "were present and knew something about it." Mr. Childs offered to submit the whole case to the public if Drs. Hawes and Spring would simply state the facts in reference to this harmonious Council. If the facts had been as Drs. H. and S. represented, then there could have been no possible objection to their being known. On the other hand, there seems to us to have been every reason why so easy and satisfactory a way for ending the controversy and silencing the objector should have been embraced. This single point must carry with it to every reflecting mind, an overwhelming force of evidence as to the real facts connected with the ordination.

present the matters which constitute disputed ground between Presbyterians and Congregationalists, and to inquire whether the Council should have proceeded to the installation of the candidate after such an avowal as is involved in the following question and answer.

Q. Suppose, sir, you were called to the death bed of an impenitent man, and knew that he had but ten minutes to live; would you tell him that he must repent and believe in Christ within that time or be lost?

A. I WOULD NOT.

Were this statement fairly made by your correspondent we should say with you, that it fully justifies the most alarming view you have taken of the case, and would have required the Council to pause before proceeding to the ordinatic But *it is not fairly made.* The question and answer are heard out of their connexion, and totally misrepresent the case. Had the Council taken the view of it thus artfully given, they would not long have deliberated, and Mr. Parker, by their act, never would have been the pastor of the South Church in Hartford. And were he to advance such a sentiment now, on a suppositious trial before his Consociation, we would be among the first to wash our hands of complicity with the error, and our suffrages for his deposition would not be lacking. We will tell you what he did say, and under what circumstances he said it.

The topic under examination was the candidate's expressed *hope* touching the *possibility* of a future state of probation for those who had never heard of Christ. In this connexion he repeatedly and distinctly said:

1. That there was no future probation for those who rejected Christ in this life. Their case was desperate and admitted of no hope.

2. That neither in the case of pagans, or unbelievers in a gospel land, would he hold out any expectation of a future state of probation.

3. That if called to the bedside of a dying pagan, or a dying man in a Christian land ignorant of Christ, and believing that he had but a short time to live, he could not shut him up to a belief in an unknown Christ or perdition. Such an one could have no sufficient intelligence of the way of salvation, and must be left in the hands of a righteous and gracious God. He WOULD NOT tell such a man that within that brief space of time he must believe in Christ or perish.

4. And in the case of a dying sinner under the light of the gospel, he would urge no other demand, and suggest no other hope than this—an immediate repentance and faith in Christ; not in nine minutes, nor five, nor one; but *now*—or you are lost!

Such were the circumstances in which that decisive answer was given. By the very circumstances in which the question was put, it and the answer were limited to the case of one ignorant of Christ. We well remember, and the Council will remember, that Mr. Parker presented in defence of his possible theory, the supposition of a youth educated in all the ignorance and crime of the "Five Points," who had never heard of the way of salvation, and yet in whose moral sensibilities there might still remain some ground for the hope that if Christ were understandingly proposed to him he would accept the Saviour. Such an one he *would not* shut up conclusively to present faith in Christ or final perdition. We do not defend or approve his views. They are repulsive to our moral sense. We had rather leave such a case where the Scriptures have left it. The Judge of all the earth will do right. We only state the facts as they can easily be recalled by every member of the Council. Any other construction than such as we have here put upon the question and answer, is at variance with the particular topic then under discussion, and in conflict with Mr. Parker's statement that for such as reject Christ there is no hope.

We know that popular favor is no certain criterion of a minister's soundness in the faith. But it is to us a somewhat significant circumstance that after a trial of five weeks or more, during which Mr. Parker had preached to a watchful church and congregation, not a few of whom are distinguished for shrewdness, intelligence, and love of the truth, he received from that people an unanimous invitation to become their pastor. They were willing themselves to sit, and to place their children, under his ministry, for his and their life, if God pleased. We have heard more than one of them declare with thankfulness their confidence that in him the great Head of the Church had sent them a teacher after his own heart. And they are not loose and careless thinkers, but men of clearsighted and far-reaching views, whose discernment and probity, and earnestness in contending for the faith, have won for them an enviable reputation in this city and its vicinage. And the examination was conducted in their presence, and in that of hundreds more—eager and interested listeners—and resulted in their entire approval, with the exception we are bound to say, of the single article already repeatedly spoken of, and which probably every member of the Council had rather not have heard.

With thanks for your former courtesy, and trusting that we may acknowledge a repetition of it in the insertion of this communication, we remain,

Your brethren in the faith,

SAMUEL SPRING.
J. HAWES.

Hartford, March 26, 1860.

To this letter the Observer added the following remarks:

REMARKS BY THE EDITORS.

1. The change of tone in this communication, from that which pervaded the former from the same venerable men, is at once remarkable and gratifying.

2. The former article censured us in severe and unwarrantable terms for giving publicity to well attested facts. The communication above furnishes as complete a vindication of the propriety of that publication as could be desired.

3. It is now evident that on most of the points in question a large majority of the Council coincided with the candidate in theological opinions.

4. On the subject of a future state of probation, the testimony of Drs. Spring and Hawes will be regarded as decisive by nineteen-twentieths of the Protestant Christian world. According to the testimony of these venerable men, the candidate held such views of the future state, that if he were called to a dying sinner ignorant of Christ, he would not shut him up to the necessity of receiving the Saviour, or of being lost. His views were, they say, "REPULSIVE TO OUR MORAL SENSE." They are so to ours. They are so to the whole Protestant Christian world, with here and there an eccentric exception. And then the question meets us: Should a man be ordained to preach the gospel whose views on a fundamental doctrine of the gospel are "repulsive to our moral sense?" Let us stand alone in the opinion, if it must be so; let the united judgment of all the Councils from that of Nice down to Hartford condemn us, but when, by holding up the right hand or saying AYE, we vote to ordain a man whose expressed sentiments are *repulsive to our moral sense*, let our right hand forget its cunning, and our tongue cleave to the roof of our mouth.

April 12th, a reply to Drs. Spring and Hawes appeared from Dr. Vermilye.

For the New York Observer.

REV. DR. VERMILYE'S STATEMENT.

HIS OWN QUESTIONS AND THE ANSWERS IN THE HARTFORD EXAMINATION.

Messrs. Editors:—At the close of my communication in regard to the Hartford ordination, it was intimated that should it become necessary, I would make a fuller statement on the subject. The recent letter of Drs. Spring and Hawes releases me from that necessity on all particulars but one, inasmuch as it concedes almost every point of any importance. I have no disposition to enter upon any controversy with them, nor to take any part in that now in progress, except to confirm what I suppose to be the truth. I may be permitted, however, to express my regret, that in a matter of so grave importance, the spirit of sectarian prejudice has been invoked, and the controversy represented as one concerning points disputed between Presbyterians and Congregationalists. I do not think that during the whole session of the council, a single question was asked or point raised, which could be so interpreted. The matters in dispute were matters of faith, not of form ; and in regard to which the standards of the two denominations are not at variance. Especially is this true of the one question which occupied so much of the time of the council.

The writers of the letter have stated that there was a solitary exception to the unanimity with which the council endorsed the candidate. It is now known that I am the person referred to. I am thankful for the kind terms in which they have been pleased to refer to me. While I have no disposition to evade any just responsibility, nor to pronounce upon that of others, it is right to say that this statement is hardly fair, if it is designed to influence public opinion, by the supposed unanimity of the council. I put it to my venerable friends, whether it is fair, not to me but to the council, and the truth, to leave the impression that they reached an easy and harmonious decision, with a single exception, or that there were only "possibly minuter shades of differing opinions?" On this very delicate subject, I have felt it my duty neither unnecessarily to proclaim nor to conceal the facts. In less than a week after the ordination, another member of the council, (with no unkind intention, I am sure,) amid a circle of ministers, made a statement similar to that which I am now considering, and named me as the single dissentient. I considered it proper then also, to protest against it, as an unfair exhibition of the facts. But I here dismiss this point. I did cast the only negative given on that occasion.

As I asserted the substantial truth of your correspondent's statements, and as this last letter charges that some of them are artfully made, and purports to refute them or explain them away, I may be excused for noticing the new points here made. I fully agree with you, Messrs. Editors, that the great and important facts are virtually admitted, and the truth of previous statements confirmed. Yet respect for my venerable friends demands, that what they regard as a satisfactory explanation should be examined. I have read, with all the candor which I can gather, this communication ; and I am constrained to say that I see no reason for altering at all my judgment of the case, or withdrawing the confirmation before given to the original statements. On all the points preceding that of future probation, there is now a fair understanding, and a substantial agreement as to what took place. Everything of any importance is virtually conceded. It seems to me, that no injustice has been done to the candidate ; I will however say, in regard to the doctrine of the Trinity, that while the statements of the letter-writer were literally true, and the candidate was not perfectly clear, my own impression, upon the whole, was, that his views were not so much positively erroneous, as defective and confused. This I said, during the session of the council, in answer to the inquiries of a friend.

Let us come now to the last, and most contested point, that of future probation. Now, in the first place, I cannot at all concede, that the whole decision turns upon the question and answer now newly expounded. The difficulty did not arise with that interrogatory, nor was it first made apparent then, nor did it even centre around it. The whole handling of this subject by the candidate was grievously unsatisfactory. Not only were his opinions virtually included in his creed; not only were they voluntarily presented, without any necessity at the point of the examination when they were brought out, as far as I could see, but they were insisted on, and elaborately defended, before this now famous question was put. I do not hesitate to affirm, that if it had never been put the case would have been a trying one to the council, and their decision would have been reached through great concern and perplexity. And if that question were now dropped out of the case, there remains a mass of evidence as to the opinion of the candidate, which cannot be easily set aside.

But we have now what purports to be a satisfactory explanation of the answer given; with the concession that if its more obvious meaning were the true one, that answer would have been a bar to the ordination. It is claimed that no other meaning than that now given is consistent with the circumstances of the case. What then is this new interpretation? It is this: that the question referred to the case of persons, pagans or others, who were in *absolute ignorance of every way of salvation*, and of the first principles of the Christian religion. It was in regard to this class of persons, actually pagan, in whatever land, that this answer was given. The phrase "ignorant of Christ" is to be taken in its most absolute sense. There is virtually but one class of persons to whom the exception involved in the answer refers. If called to the bedside of a *dying pagan*, in India, or New York, the candidate would not shut him up to the necessity of finding Christ as his Saviour, or being left without hope.

Now with all respect for my venerable brethren, I will state why I cannot accept the interpretation thus given. I claim a right to speak with some certainty as to the real object of the question, because it was framed and put by myself, during that part of the examination which I conducted. It was deliberately and carefully stated to the candidate with all necessary explanations. It was designedly put as an extreme case, to test the practical effect of his theory, in his ministry. It was put not as a general question, but to him individually as the supposed pastor of the South Church in Hartford; and the point was not what it might be *expedient* to do, but what would *he feel justified in saying,* doctrinally, if it were expedient to state such an alternative. It was put as significant of the last lingering hope in my own mind, that the candidate might be extricated from his unhappy position, though of course with the ruin of his consistency. The answer did not surprise me : it was in the direct line of his previous statements : and on hearing it, I surrendered the case as hopeless, so far as I was concerned. Now I claim that I ought to have known the bearing and relations of my own question; and at the risk of being considered a witness in my own case, I affirm that the candidate ought not to have misunderstood it. Nor can any advantage justly be taken of the "Five Points" illustration, or of the ambiguity of the phrase "ignorant of Christ." For as to the former, the question was partly framed to carry the candidate beyond such cases ; and as to the latter, I distinctly said in substance, "I mean a man who has intelligence enough to understand you, and who, finding himself suddenly in the face of death, sends for you to tell him how he may save his soul." It is said, that any other than the new interpretation is inconsistent with the circumstances of the case. But how is the exclamation of Dr. Hawes (substantially)—"then the man will never repent, if you give him any time beyond the present life,"—consistent with the new view, or with the "shutting up a man to a belief in an unknown Christ, or perdition," which I am supposed to have demanded ? The application of my question to the literal pagan is absolutely untenable. No such application was in my thoughts. The question was personal and practical—"What would *you* do ?" —and the pastor of the South Church in Hartford is not likely to be called to the dying bed of a literal pagan. This view of the case also represents Mr. Parker as cherishing the hope of a future probation for all the heathen indiscriminately. But if the application of the question be confined to the supposed virtuous heathen, they were expressly remitted to a more hopeful condition. For when the attempt was made, by the kindness of one of Mr. P.'s friends in the council, to reduce the whole case to this category, and to make him admit that his scruples referred only to those of whom, for example, Socrates was a type, the reply was, "No, Sir ; that is not it at all ; I believe Socrates went to heaven." Of course, he needed no further probation. I must repeat, that the case of the dying pagan was absolutely excluded from my question. Nor did it apply to the case of one dying in a christian land in entire ignorance on the subject of religion. Indeed it seemed to me, that the true application was conceded in the first defence offered. The excuse for the unhappy answer then alleged was, not that it applied to a man in pagan or semi-pagan darkness, but that "he would not broach the supposition, in public or in private, to an impenitent man." Need I say what is the common meaning of the phrase, "an impenitent man?"

But did he not say, that for those who *rejected* Christ there was no hope? I will not *deny* that he did; though the sentiment was not as clearly presented to my mind as it seems to have been to others. Still I will yield to their clearer convictions. But I can only say, that I was compelled to think that he referred to a class of persons, who deliberately and obstinately repudiated this way of salvation. For them there was no hope. Another class consisted of those who were utterly "ignorant of Christ:" for these he hoped for a future probation. Another class consisted of impenitent men; such as many of those who hear the word. These he would not shut up absolutely in a dying hour, to a reception of Christ, or perdition. My venerable friends now say that he would. They affirm for him, the very thing which to me he denied.

And now, Messrs. Editors, I believe with you, that the case is given up by your correspondents, in their very statement of it.—Why would not Mr. Parker shut up a dying sinner, a dying pagan, if you please, to faith in Christ, or perdition? He certainly would not rest on the paltry evasion that "ten minutes" was not long enough to teach him: for no stress was laid upon the time, except that it was "*a short time*," as your correspondents say; and the measure of it was varied. He will not seriously say, that I asked him to shut a man up to faith in an unknown Christ. Let us brush away the fog. Would he *make known* to a dying man "ignorant of Christ," that Christ is his *only* hope of salvation? "If called to the death-bed of an impenitent man, who had but a short time to live, would he tell him that he must repent and believe in Christ, *within that time*,—before he died,—or be lost?" He said he would not. I think he meant so: and his reason was found in his hope of a future state of probation. And the mind is not relieved, but the more perplexed, by the "Five Points" illustration. As has been said before, the "question" went beyond that case, intention-•ally. But what is the meaning of the language, "in whose moral sensibilities there might still remain some ground for the hope that if Christ were understandingly proposed to him, he would accept the Saviour?" I should interpret it to apply to one, who, as was said of some of the heathen, might have the spirit of faith, but to whom the object of faith was not made known. But these would be regenerate persons, and, like Socrates, would go directly to heaven! A member of the council said to me, that he understood the candidate to deny the doctrine of original sin. Will that furnish the explanation? I fear the true explanation must be found in Mr. P.'s declaration, when asked a reason for his views, that he felt as if God would give every one a "fair chance." I am afraid that the vague and general interpretation which has been given, cannot hide the true meaning of that unfortunate expression. It was uttered in the connection I have indicated. It revealed to my mind, at least, the source of all the young pastor's difficulties, in the principle that God's mercy would not permit him to cast off any who had not deliberately rejected the way of salvation through Christ. Every one must have a *"fair chance."*

My venerable friends will bear with me in so long a letter; the more as it is now publicly known, that no one else in the council will be likely to annoy them with any further remonstrance. I had no agency in bringing this matter before the public, and only spoke under an apparent necessity And I might be permitted now, perhaps, to say a word as to my personal relations to the council, and the examination of the candidate. I took my seat, with the intention to ask no question myself; and every one put by me was in kindness, and with the purpose, if possible, of satisfying my own mind of his substantial soundness. When I found myself alone in the negative, I considered myself exonerated, and my personal duty at an end. But it is far more important than any personal matters to say, that we may believe that the truth will be promoted and good accomplished by this discussion. The irritation of feeling on the part of brethren will pass away. The trouble and annoyance which have been experienced by the young pastor, and by his friends in his church and elsewhere, will be forgotten; if, at least, he shall prove himself a faithful teacher of the truth, and shall vindicate the charitable judgment of the council in his case. But this is gained. We have the unequivocal declaration of Drs. Spring and Hawes, for themselves and the council, that had they understood Mr. Parker to hold what he was supposed by some to hold, they would have refused him ordination; and even now would vote for his deposition. We have also their judgment that what he did avow on this important point, is erroneous, and "repulsive to their moral sense." This is enough; they will not now be quoted as holding or sanctioning any modified views on this topic. If any have been disposed to defend Mr. Parker's views, or if Universalists have been anxious to claim him, as in the first steps of the road towards their encampment,—let it be distinctly understood that the fathers of the churches pronounce those supposed views to be "heresy," and severely condemn the "laxity" with which the young pastor is really chargeable. Let it be distinctly understood that orthodox councils will not sanction such deviations from the truth. If this shall be gained, I shall be content to be supposed to have erred in my solitary vote.

East Windsor Hill, Ct.　　　　　ROBT. G. VERMILYE.

Mr. Parker himself then appeared in the Observer of April 19th :—

MR. PARKER'S LETTER.

REV. E. P. PARKER, ON HIS EXAMINATION FOR OR-DINATION AT HARTFORD, CONN.

HARTFORD, April 13, 1860.

To the Editors of the New York Observer:

Until I read the letter of Dr. Vermilye, (Observer, April 12,) I had strong hopes that a fair statement of the facts in the case would satisfactorily explain to him my position at the Hartford ordination. I now neither hope nor care to satisfy him. I only wish to make a few remarks, state the facts, and leave the truth to God. I have in my possession elaborate articles from men who attended the examination and *carefully noted down my positions*, in which are statements irreconcilable with those of Mr. Childs, or with the limping logic of Dr. Vermilye. I now forbear to publish them, being quite convinced that such a course would only tend to protract a disgusting controversy. In regard to Dr. Vermilye's letter I beg leave to make the following remarks.

(1.) It is merely a specious and repetitious plea *for his own forced construction* of a question, which without any *intelligible* explanation, was put to me by him at the examination. It is quite remarkable that, according to this letter, that question was purposely framed so as to *meet* and *obviate* all other possible constructions.— The thing is slightly overdone we think!

(2.) No such explanation as he says "in substance" he gave, fell on my ears.

(3.) Whatever the real object of the question may have been, as it revolved in the interrogator's mind, the council and candidate could but interpret the question for themselves. If Dr. V. had any such object in asking the question as he labors to state, that object was unhinted by him in the question itself. I answered the question and "claim a right to speak with some certainty as to the" obvious *meaning* of the question.

(4.) In neither of the letters written by Dr. Vermilye has he given my answer to his question. Mr. Childs has given a part of it, but only the flexible part. The answer was, "I would not, but WOULD *tell him of Christ!*"

(5.) I indignantly *deny* that I voluntarily presented my perplexities on this matter to the council. On the other hand, an acknowledgment of them was *screwed* out of me by Dr. Hawes and others. I distinctly told the council that I thought an examination on this *mere doubt* was unfair!

I also *deny* that I defended on any ground a belief in a future probation *for any*. I never had any such *belief.* I never expressed any such belief.

(6.) I am happy to state that Drs. Hawes and Spring very much lament an unaccountable slip of the pen in their last article. They intended to say—"the views ascribed *by Mr. Childs* to Mr. Parker were repulsive to their moral sense!" In the hurry of writing or recasting their article they omitted a part of what they intended to say. Therefore, all the clever patronage with which Dr. V.'s letter so complacently closes, is so much waste ink.

(7.) I ever have, still do, and pray God I ever shall believe, that God will give all men "*a fair chance!*" I *know* he will.

(8.) The construction now put upon "the awful question," and most triumphantly *arrogated* throughout this letter, is, in view of the connection in which the question was put, an unnatural and illogical one; and (if I may be allowed to look up towards the East Windsor Hill with the least bit of levity) at once reminded me of the old song—"When a twister a-twisting will twist him a twist, &c."!

Let me now state the facts in the case.

I pass by the questions on "Inspiration," "Trinity," and "Ability," not because, as is *modestly assumed*, the charges of Mr. Childs are conceded to be true—for I claim that they are false charges—but because the whole discussion has been hinged on the single subject of future probation.

And first, let us compare the original charge with the one now insisted on. I extract from your columns of the 23d of February. "He (the candidate) *held* that after death * * * there is a state for all souls * * * where some *who had rejected Christ in this life* would have a new offer of Christ and salvation." *Now* the charge is that the candidate said—" *I incline to the belief*" that after death, &c. And the words "rejected Christ in this life" are omitted! Which of these charges were [was?] made from "*those notes,*" we are not informed. For the progress towards truth, however, we should be grateful.*

But let us take the more guarded charge, which is nearest truth. "*I incline to the belief,*" &c.

The answer of which these words are the beginning was not given at all, to a question concerning salvation in a future state; but only to a question concerning my views in regard *to the fact* of an intermediate state of the dead. I was requested to state my views on this point, and I said—"I incline to the belief that there is a state or condition after death for all souls," and then added that I rather inclined to the opinion that this intermediate state would be the lot of all the dead until the resurrection, when the righteous would enter upon the consummate bliss, being incorporate, and the wicked depart into their full measure of woe. I said that my mind was as *yet unsettled* on this point. Now the question of the *possibility* of *salvation* in this state was an after question. It had no logical connection whatever with the words, "I incline to

---

* This reflection would have been saved, if the writer had noticed that the Observer in this remark, did not profess to quote the words either of the Letter or the notes.

the belief." I did not say, *at any time* during the examination that I *believed*, or "inclined to the belief" that some souls would have a new offer of salvation in Hades. "I inclined to a belief" in an intermediate state. (See Note I. below.) As to what I *did* say:' Throughout the whole discussion on that memorable day, I limited the bare possibility of future probation to such as had never *heard* or *known* of Christ. I repeatedly remarked that for such as rejected Christ in this life there was nothing to support a conjecture of future probation. (See Note II. below.) On this point I felt no perplexity. In regard to such as had never had any knowledge of religious things, I said in substance this: "The Bible does not make it decisive and unquestionable to me, that the eternal state of every human soul will be fixed at death." I said that the whole Bible *looked* that way; that it gave *me no reliable evidence* that there would be a probation *for any* after death. Consequently I said I had no such belief. In the general and awful silence of the Bible I simply listened to the echoes of my own quick heart-beats, while thinking on the matter. Dr. Lawrence, with his characteristic kindness, quoted a certain passage, and remarked in tones that fell strangely sweet into that hoarser confusion of voices, that he doubted not the candidate by a prayerful study of that passage would come to be wholly relieved *of his perplexity.*

I am sorry to contradict Dr. Vermilye and Mr. Childs—but am glad to say that I *did not* defend the belief in a future probation. I *did not* quote a verse from the Epistle of Peter in support of such a theory. I said that this passage had been used by eminent men in the church to support the doctrine, but that *it did* NOT *satisfy me!** (See Note 3d below.) I will add that considerable ingenuity was displayed by one member of the council in an apparent attempt to force me to some extreme position on what I repeatedly told him was a doubtful, unsettled point in my mind. We come now to the awful question. What Dr. Vermilye's aim was in asking the question, nobody knows but himself. I can modestly return his compliment and assure him that his letter is "grievously unsatisfactory" on this point. I thought I knew what the question fairly should mean, when it was put; though at the time it was generally considered a remarkable, rather than an appropriate question. There are one or two versions of this labored question. We will take Mr. Childs' version. I most solemnly affirm that the question *was asked* in connection with an *outcast* from the "Five Points" who had no knowledge of Christ. The question rested squarely on that basis. It was generally so understood. (See note 4th below.) Observe that only a *part* of my answer to this question has yet been given. The answer was this —"I would not, *but would tell him of Christ!*" Now the question was in substance this, "would you, if called to the death bed of

---

* Compare with this the statement of Dr. Spring in the Expositor, p. 11.

an impenitent man (who had no knowledge of Christ, or who had been brought up in ignorance of religious things) who had but ten minutes to live, tell him he must repent and believe on Christ within that time or be lost?" *Answer*—"I would not, *but would tell him of Christ.*" I insist that this is the true light in which to view the question. This is the light in which nine-tenths of those present did view it, whatever obscure purpose the questioner may have had.

Well, I am made to appear as answering, "I would not in my instructions shut a man up to immediate repentance and faith;" whereas I own that the Bible hems us all in to immediate reconciliation, and would myself follow the leading of the Bible *implicitly* in this respect. But the ictus of the question fell on the word "tell!" Would you "tell" such a man that he must believe in ten minutes or be damned. "I would not," &c. "Would not" what? Why, would not place any such alternative before such a man. It would be just such spiritual angling as Bellamy reproved a student for. Said he—"You toss your great hook in and say *"Bite or be damned!"* No sirs! I would not tell such a soul any such thing. Why did **Dr.** Vermilye say *"ten* minutes" if he objects to sticking to it? Such a man, I would above all pray for with all my might. Then I would tell him of Jesus if possibly I might just *introduce* him to the Saviour, or the Saviour to him. That is what I would do. That is what I said I would do. To a man who had previously rejected Christ I would say—Not ten, or five, or two minutes but *now!* You have not the shadow of a hope beyond *just now!* This sirs, is the true interpretation of the question and answer. If, Dr. V. asked the question and so ought to know about it, I answered it and was more interested in it. I should answer the question as then put and understood, in the same way, if it should be put to me again. "Would you shut him up?" This is another thing; what do you mean by this? Would I pass judgment on him? No! Would I, in my instructions, flash the terrors of hell-fire before his face? No! Would I close every door on him to which I had access, *but that of faith in Christ? Yes I would!* Thus the Bible shuts men up, and thus I would do it always! But neither I nor you, nor any but God has a right otherwise to shut up a dying soul. *I would environ* a soul with the necessity of immediate repentance and faith, but as for dropping it into hell, if I saw no evidence of its repentance, why I never would do it. I would leave it with God and follow it with—— fears? hopes? doubts? yes, but above all with *faith in God!**

---

* What is the meaning of this? Mr. Parker would not drop into hell a soul in whom he saw no evidence of repentance! Does he mean solemnly to assure the public that he is not the Eternal Judge? The public needed no such assurance. Does he mean to say that for a man who has died with no evidence of repentance, he has no ground to decide whether he is sealed to perdition? Does he mean to say that he sees no inevitable connection between an impenitent death bed and eternal woe? We

Is that heresy? Then put a cross against my name, or brand the black mark of heresy upon the yet soft cheek of my character and I will wear it as an ornament! I said in substance before the council, what Mr. Childs would have me say—though I suppose he otherwise understood me—that "Christ believed on *now*" is the only reliable ground of hope. The Bible surveys no other ground for us. There and then I declared I should be thus compelled to preach; and would I have promised to preach what I did not believe? Dr. Vermilye says "He will not seriously say that I asked him to shut a man up to faith in an unknown Christ!" I do say with all respect, that if the question in its connection *meant anything at all*, that *was what it did mean!* Would I tell a man who had been brought up in *utter ignorance* of religious things, who had but so many minutes to live, to believe in Christ or he would be eternally damned? It would be neither justifiable nor expedient. I will leave the matter here. I can state my views on this subject when courteously asked, or ecclesiastically summoned so to do. At present, cheered by many messages from various quarters in New England, blessed with kindest encouragements even from *one* who came from East Windsor Hill to my examination, and with perfect unanimity sustained by my church, I prefer to listen and wait, after having thus explained my views as stated to the council.— And now, to show you that I have evidence of what I say, allow me to present the following notes in order, *copied from the private note-book of* Dr. Samuel Harris, where they written by him immediately after reaching home after examination.*

Dr. Harris' statements were written independently of mine of course. He says, "I am sure that Mr. Childs has not obtained a correct idea of Mr. Parker's actual belief; and that *every one of his seven specifications* is either an incorrect or inadequate representation of Mr. P.'s doctrine on the point. In many instances your correspondent has *omitted important statements* actually made by the candidate, which prove his doctrine widely different from that ascribed to him." Now as to the notes. *Note 1st.* Dr. Harris says, "I distinctly remember the remark, 'I incline to the belief,' and also that the subject respecting which he said it, *was not* the question whether there will be any offer of mercy after death, but the *general subject* of an intermediate state of the dead." *Note 2d.* Dr.

---

think he does. For he would follow such a soul not only with "fears," but with "hopes!" not only with "doubts" but with "faith in God!" Hopes of what? and faith for what? What, but the mercy of God? and where, but beyond the grave? These are significant words. To our mind they reveal the spring from which all that has been affirmed of Mr. Parker's faith could come.

* These notes bear such unmistakable evidence of reference to the controversy as it was in progress, that Mr. Parker must be in error in supposing them written immediately after the ordination. Of course the reference to Mr. Childs was not then written; the expression "your correspondent" seems quite unintelligible; and the words in *Note 1st*, "I distinctly remember the remark, &c.," obviously refer to a remark in Mr. Childs' letter.

Harris says, "Mr. P. declared that he felt sure that there will be no offer of mercy in the future life to such as have had the gospel in this life." *Note 3d.* Dr. H. says, "He (candidate) had examined 1st Peter, 3 : 19, and was satisfied it *does not prove* that there will be probation to *any* after death. He was convinced that there is no reliable evidence in the Bible, justifying a belief in a probation after death."

Note 4th. "The case being supposed of *an outcast* in the Five Points, in N. Y. city, who *had never heard* of Christ, the question was asked, If called to such a person, knowing that he had but ten minutes to live, &c. The answer was, I would not, but would tell him of Christ."* I could quote more fully and conclusively from these notes, had I time and room.

There remains only this to be added : Drs. Hawes and Spring fully endorse these notes of Prof. Harris, as a fair representation of the case. I forbear to quote, except upon the most important points. A dozen men who heard the examination have told me that they could heartily subscribe to these my statements. In fact 29-30ths of those present at that examination would join in affirming these same things. Allow me, in closing, to express my deep regret that this controversy has arisen. In a strange land, *such a* publicity has been a source of grievous suffering to me. Nor would it be delicate for me to expose the severer wounds which these weekly arrows, unwittingly winged, have made in the tenderer heart of one of far dearer to me than even my reputation. If there may be a peaceable close of this controversy, I pray that it may speedily come. I hereby call upon all aggrieved persons rather than to prosecute any longer a war with these paper bullets, to call me to some face-to-face account, that the matter may be settled.

Am I guilty of heresy? I wish to know it. Do I preach the ministry of reconciliation, rightly dividing the word of God? I wish to do it, unbespattered and unsuspected.

Towards Mr. Childs I have not the slightest ill-feeling. I think he is mistaken; and had he consulted with me I think we could have come more nearly together. That God will speedily bring this matter to a settlement, that he will guide all who have taken part in this discussion into truth, and keep them in good faith and temper, and more especially thus bless Mr. Childs, the Eds. of Observer, Dr. Vermilye and myself, is my sincere prayer.

Very respectfully,   EDWIN POND PARKER.

---

*In regard to this addition to the answer. (1.) If Drs. Hawes and Spring had heard it, it is very remarkable that they make no reference to it in any of their replies. (2.) We have the direct evidence of Dr. Vermilye and Mr. Childs that they did not hear it, and Dr. Vermilye was the gentleman to whom the answer was given, if it was given at all. (3.) The answer is utterly inconsistent with the admitted exclamation of Dr. Hawes. According to this statement Mr. Parker says 'I would tell the dying sinner of Christ,' and Dr. Hawes exclaims, 'then he will never repent'—a very remarkable logical inference !

This letter was accompanied by the following editorial com-ments:—

REMARKS BY THE EDITORS.

The little flings in the first paragraph of Mr. Parker's letter must be excused on account of the writer's youth, and not be allowed to weaken the force of his argument.

Mr. Parker must have misapprehended Drs. Spring and Hawes, if they have attempted to explain to him personally their remarks respecting his views. Their language is this:

"We well remember, and the Council will remember, that Mr. Parker presented in defence of his possible theory, the supposition of a youth educated in all the ignor-ance and crime of the "Five Points," who had never heard of the way of salvation, and yet in whose moral sensibilities there might still remain some ground for the hope that if Christ were understandingly proposed to him he would accept the Saviour. Such an one he *would not* shut up conclusively to present faith in Christ or final per-dition. We do not defend or approve his views. They are repulsive to our moral sense. We had rather leave such a case where the Scriptures have left it. The judge of all the earth will do right. We only state the facts as they can easily be recalled by every member of the Council."

No "slip of the pen" and no "omission" can make this language refer to anything but the views that Mr. Parker expressed. Drs. Spring and Hawes declare "we do not defend or approve his views. They are repulsive to our moral sense." And so they are to the Christian Church.

Mr. Parker is needlessly sensitive respecting the discussion as if it mainly concerned *him*. He mistakes the point entirely. It is not what *he* believes, that the public "cares" to know. The *coun-cil*, not the candidate, is now before the public. The question is "what did the candidate profess to believe, or not believe *when un-der examination*." Perhaps he failed to express his sentiments, and all we have sought to learn is now sufficiently proved by the letters of Messrs. Spring, Hawes, Vermilye and Childs, who have satisfied all intelligent minds as to the facts in the case. With the facts before them, the Council ordained a candidate whose views on a vital point in the gospel they do not "defend or approve." If nothing else is settled, that is.

Mr. Parker's letter makes but one addition to the testimony. In reply to the question, would you shut a dying sinner up to &c., he said "I would not." So the witnesses have told us. He now adds "*I would tell him of Christ*," as part of his answer. This additional clause does not help the case. *What* would you tell him of Christ? Would you tell him he must now believe or perish? If you be-*lieved* so, you would tell him so: if you do not believe so, you would not preach the gospel to that poor sinner. But the exclama-tion of Dr. Hawes shows clearly that this additional clause was not heard by the Council. It is in evidence that when Mr. P. re-plied, "I would not," Dr. Hawes exclaimed, "*Then he would never repent!*" Now we repeat the reply in the new form proposed, "No, I would not: I would tell him of Christ." And Dr. Hawes exclaims: "Then he would never repent," a remark that would be very extraordinary after the answer suggested.

Mr. Parker must divest himself of the idea that the public has anything to do with him. Let him by a faithful, zealous, and scriptural exhibition of the Gospel, show to his people and to the Church at large, that his views have been totally misapprehended: that he regards with abhorrence the idea that the heathen may repent and believe after they are dead : that he does not hold even the sentiments which the council believed him to hold when they ordained him; and this unpleasant affair will not be a damage; it will be a great blessing to him.

Here, we trust, this particular discussion will be suffered to rest. Other cases and other subjects demand our space and attention.— We have great reason to bless God that *this* matter has been brought up and has arrested so widely the attention of the churches. The discussion has already done vast good. The development has satisfied the most incredulous that there is far more ground for anxiety than they supposed. Orthodox ministers will be more careful and watchful and faithful. Theological teachers have had a new lesson to learn, by which they will not fail to improve. And we have been taught to be more vigilant, earnest and outspoken in defence of the *evangelical* doctrines of our holy religion.

----------◆----------

April 26th the Observer closed the controversy with the following notes :—

For the New York Observer.

DRS. SPRING AND HAWES.

Messrs. Editors:—We had not intended to draw upon your indulgence, or the patience of your readers, any further. But the construction put upon one expression, in our last communication, requires a brief notice. We then said, "We do not defend, or approve his (Mr. Parker's) views. They are repulsive to our moral sense." This remark, you, and your respected correspondent at East Windsor, will perceive was expressly limited to a suppositious case, and furnishes no ground for the premature triumph that we have "yielded the main points at issue." And we may be permitted to claim the privilege of interpreting our own admission. It was not that Mr. Parker's avowed belief—including his creed, and his examination as a whole—was repulsive, but that on this particular point he put forth a suggestion—or rather a hope, not a belief —which we could not adopt, and which if interpreted as had been done, and we thought unfairly, would have furnished valid reason for his rejection by the Council. Enough had been said, in various parts of both of our communications, to exempt us from the charge of endorsing even his cautious and modified speculations on the subject of a possible, future probation. A fair, and, as we intended, the only, construction that could be put upon our admission is, that his views, *as interpreted by your first correspondent*, are obnoxious, and would, if so understood by us, have been a bar to our further progress in the ordination. The words used by us may *seem* to imply more than this; but then they would be totally at variance with what we have elsewhere abundantly asserted; and our brethren will, we think, hardly allege that we have been so grossly inconsistent as in the same communication to have perpetrated so stolid a contradiction. We regret that our decided condemnation of the construction put upon Mr. Parker's views by his critics, should have been deemed a condemnation of the candidate's belief. We should have indeed stultified ourselves, and have deserved at once to forfeit the confidence of the churches, if such a charge could be righteously alleged. And how our brethren, who say they respect us, can admit such a reflection, we are not a little perplexed to understand.

Respectfully yours,

SAMUEL SPRING,
J. HAWES.

That the intelligent reader may have the connection in which the remark, now explained, was made, we subjoin the whole paragraph from the former letter of Drs. Spring and Hawes.—*Eds. of Obs.*

"Such were the circumstances in which that decisive answer was given. By the very circumstances in which the question was put, it and the answer were limited to the case of one ignorant of Christ. We well remember, and the council will remember, that Mr. Parker presented, in defence of his possible theory, the supposition of a youth, educated in all the ignorance and crime of the " Five Points," who had never heard of the way of salvation, and yet in whose moral sensibilities there might still remain some ground for the hope that if Christ were understandingly proposed to him he would accept the Saviour. Such an one he *would not* shut up conclusively to present faith in Christ or final perdition. We do not defend or approve his views. They are repulsive to our moral sense. We had rather leave such a case where the Scriptures have left it. The Judge of all the earth will do right. We only state the facts as they can easily be recalled by every member of the council. Any other construction than such as we have here put upon the question and answer, is at variance with the particular topic then under discussion, and in conflict with Mr. Parker's statement that for such as reject Christ there is no hope."

For the New York Observer.

REV. MR. CHILDS.

Messrs. Editors:—I shall not burden you with a long communication. The statements of both sides are before the world. I re-affirm the truth of my original letter. As to the only point now at issue, if it be understood that *not to receive* an offered Christ is to *reject* him, the controversy is at an end.

My object now is to correct a single statement in the last letter of Drs. Hawes and Spring. The rest we can afford to pass. In their substitution of remarkable personalities for facts and arguments, they say, " Your correspondent has been admitted, with all kindness, and without the suspicion that he would make any other than a friendy and honorable use of the confidence thus reposed in him, to the most unreserved disclosures which his brethren of three denominations in the city have made of their views," &c.

The reference is to certain informal meetings of the pastors of different churches in the city; and the implication is, that, in this controversy, I have made a dishonorable use of information received at these meetings. To this my reply is—(1.) I do not accept ministerial fellowship from any man as a favor. (2.) The ordination of Mr. Parker took place in January last. I have not attended one of the meetings referred to since that time, nor for more than a year previous. This Dr. Hawes *knew* when he signed the letter. (3.) I made use of no information in my statements and proofs, that was not given to the public on the open examination of Mr. Parker.*   Truly yours,

T. S. CHILDS.

Hartford, April 21, 1860.

In the Presbyterian Expositor of May 17th, Mr. Childs replied to Dr. Spring as follows:

---

* The endeavor of Drs. Hawes and Spring to break the force of Mr. Childs' testimony, in the manner referred to in the above note, deserves a much severer reply than Mr. C. has given it. As the meetings in question were gatherings of Hartford pastors, Dr. Spring could have known nothing of them personally, and had no right to bear witness in the case. As they were *mutual* gatherings, it was as much a favor to Dr. Hawes to be "admitted" to them, as to Mr. Childs. There was no favor in the case, and the claim is pure arrogance. But the thing assumes a worse aspect in view of the fact that Mr. Childs *had entirely withdrawn from these meetings* more than a year before the present events, and that that Dr. Hawes knew it!

So far, therefore, from having made a dishonorable use of information received, Mr. Childs has confined himself carefully to facts which were fairly open to the public, and to which the public was fully entitled.

43

THE HARTFORD ORDINATION.

Rev. Dr. Rice—*Dear Sir:*—I have refrained from noticing the letter of Dr. Spring, in regard to the above subject, which appeared in the Expositor of March 15th, preferring to wait till the evidence was in. As the controversy seems closed, I may now claim that every point in the letter which appeared in the Expositor of Feb. 23d, is either admitted or clearly proved. On the one point on which the defenders of the Council took their last stand—namely, that of probation after death—it is clearly admitted by Drs. Hawes and Spring, that there were *some* impenitent persons to whom the candidate was supposed to be ministering on a death bed, whom he would not shut up to a present faith in Christ as the only hope of salvation. If, (as Dr. Spring I presume constantly teaches,) not to receive an offered Saviour *is* to reject him, then he has granted the only point of the letter, which he undertook to refute. In view of the facts of the case, it is not easy to reconcile either with justice or Christian courtesy, his strong statements that my communication "conveys an impression *totally at variance with the truth*," and that I have "either stolidly misapprehended or wilfully misrepresented his (the candidate's) views." The fact is, the worst aspect of this whole case is not yet before the public; and with the exception of one point, it is not an uncommon case. I had heard the public examination of a member of this same council who was himself all unsettled as to a state of eternal punishment for any. Another member had declared on his examination, that there were parts of the Bible which were not inspired—had denied the Scripture doctrine of original sin—and asserted that man had natural ability to repent and believe independent of Christ and the Holy Spirit; and still another has recently said, while preaching in a *Universalist* pulpit, that "he hoped the day would come—and that day was not far distant—when all Christian denominations would overcome their prejudices, and be willing to listen to the preaching of any Christian minister without sacrificing their own ideas upon religious matters;" a sentiment, which, if it meant anything, distinctly recognized the christian character and equal standing of Universalism. I have it also from a responsible source, that a member of this council has publicly, in his pulpit, given thanks to God that there were such denominations as the Universalist and Unitarian, to modify the views others have of God. It stands uncontradicted that five of the students of Andover, last year, lapsed into Universalism. In these cases we have representatives from three of the Theological schools of New England, viz: Bangor, New Haven, and Andover. These are fearful facts. As a New England man, I have no pleasure, but profound grief in stating them. How such good men as Dr.

Spring, can look upon them with indifference—how in view of the awful issues involved, and their own near judgment, they can ever appear as the defenders of those who hold any such views, is to me amazing.

In regard to the statements of the *Congregationalist*, which refer to me as the author of the exposures of the New England theology, they give me too much credit. In the first place the exposures began long before I had entered the ministry. In the second place, until this ordination I do not remember to have written an article for the papers, except two or three brief ones upon other subjects, for several years. Whether the facts in this case were such as to justify their publication will be judged differently, according as men value the truth of God. Yours truly,

T. S. Childs.

Hartford, Ct., May 5, 1860.

Review.

In regard to the issue of the foregoing controversy we suppose there can hardly be two opinions. The defence has clearly failed. They have failed, in the first place, to convict the author of the original Letter of one of the charges, touching his veracity or his honor, which they had laid against him. In this view their strong denials and bitter personalities are quite unjustifiable.* In religious controversy there is much in the spirit with which it is conducted. A bad spirit is presumptive evidence of a bad cause. No man is called of God to defend His truth to whom He does not give some portion of His spirit for the work. On the other hand, when a man gives himself up to error or to the defence of error, it is in accordance with the Divine dealings that he should be given up to a corresponding temper.

The endeavor to invalidate Mr. Childs' testimony, by a reference to his ecclesiastical position, seems to us neither relevant nor fair. The whole community were invited to attend Mr. Parker's examination, that they might judge of his qualifications for the office to which he had been called. If the result had been favorable, and Mr. P. had passed a satisfactory examination, there would have

---

* Upon this point the *Boston Recorder*, which will not be accused of partiality towards Mr. Childs, says, (April 12th) :—"Drs. Spring and Hawes have appeared in a letter of nearly two closely printed columns, in explanation of the course which they took as members of the ordaining Council, and illustrative of their own views upon the general case. In the course of their communication they speak frequently, and in terms which appear to us stronger than were called for by the circumstances, of the improper spirit of the author of the first Letter. Their language is, in several instances, such as if taken in its full meaning, would bring on him an odium which we do not think his course, in the present matter, at all deserves, and we believe the great Christian public are with us in this opinion. With Mr. Childs we have no acquaintance except what has grown out of this single affair,—we have never seen him, and till very recently, we did not know whether he was a minister or a layman, a Presbyterian or a Congregationalist. We have looked upon the case from outside the circle of excitement, and have endeavored to judge of it candidly, and in the fear of Him who tries the hearts of men, and our judgment is, that while Mr. Childs has written earnestly, he is not to be charged with a perverse spirit, or a desire to do wrong to Christian brethren. Truth on points like those which come into the questions raised by this discussion, is important, and worth defending, and a good degree of earnestness should be allowed to a writer without incurring the charge of perverseness of spirit, or a disposition to accuse or find fault with his brethren."

been no objection to its being published by any man, as widely as he saw fit. Why, then, should there be any objection when the result was different? Surely the public were not less interested in it; nor was it less important that the truth should be known. If the facts were as stated, we put it to every candid man, whether it would not have been perfectly competent for *any* person who was present, to give them to the public; and if a Presbyterian minister, in answer to a request from a Congregational brother, writes his honest impressions in regard to the examination, and that brother believes the letter sufficiently important to justify its publication, it would seem quite unworthy grave and venerable men, to meet its statements by proclaiming the ecclesiastical position of the writer.

That the case is one in which publicity was justifiable will now hardly be questioned. It was a public act of a public Council; from which, it is to be remembered, there is no appeal except to the public. The propriety of such appeal, if the statements were correct, was granted by the parties and papers which have most earnestly taken the side of the defence. The "specifications and proofs" were demanded.* · It was insisted, "that if there *is* such unsoundness among us, the Christian public have a right to know *the facts.*"† This is correct; and we can hardly reconcile it with these demands, or with good faith to the public, or with fairness to the parties concerned, or with fidelity to the truth, that, when the "specifications and proofs" which they had demanded were given, and the "facts" established, these papers should have entirely refused to give them to the public.

The defence has failed in regard to the subject matter of the controversy. The statements of the original Letter are maintained. Mr. Parker did deny the verbal inspiration of the Scriptures; he was not clear on the Trinity; he rejected the common doctrine of Original Sin; he affirmed the ability of sinners to fulfil the commands of God; he maintained that the gospel was not absolutely necessary to the salvation of adult heathen; he held that Christ died with the same *design* for all men; and he inclined to the belief that for some who died impenitent there was a future state of probation. These were the points stated in Mr. Childs' letter; and we think it will be generally agreed that every one of them has not only been proved, but has been really admitted by the defence. It is admitted, on all hands, that Mr. Parker rejected the verbal inspiration of the Scriptures; it is in uncontroverted evidence that he was not clear on the Trinity—his own written creed showing that he so far "doubted as to the use of the word *person*" as to entirely suppress it. It is admitted by all, that he denied holiness as pertaining to the nature of God, and sinfulness as pertaining to the nature of man; it is admitted that he maintained the sinner's ability, in the sense of 'adequate power,' to fulfil the commands of God; it is admitted that he held that some heathen (as Socrates for example,) have gone to heaven without the gospel; it is in evidence, and undenied, that he said that "Christ died with the same design for Judas Iscariot as for Paul;" it is admitted that there were *some* impenitent persons to whom Mr. Parker was supposed to be ministering on a death bed, whom he would not shut up to a present faith in Christ as the only hope of salvation.

All these points but the last are really yielded, not only in detail but in a mass, in the second communication of Drs. Spring and Hawes. In regard to the last point, while Mr. Parker is to be allowed the benefit of his present statements for himself, this can not set aside the whole body of testimony as to the action of the Council. In all that testimony there is not the slightest intimation, until we come to Mr. Parker's letter, that the "famous question" referred to the propriety of *a certain form of speech* to be used to a dying man. Neither Drs. Harris, Hawes or Spring undertake any such defence as that. Everything shows that the examination was on no such trifling matter as that. Dr. Vermilye was not asking Mr. Parker whether "in his instructions, he would flash the terrors of hell fire before the man's face;" he was not asking him if he "would pass judgment" on him; he was asking him if he would shut the sinner up to a present faith in Christ as the only hope of salvation! Mr. P. now says "I would close every door on him to which I had access, but that of faith in Christ." Why does he say "*to which I had access?*" Does it intimate that there was a door to which he had not access, and which, therefore, he had no right to close? This is in accordance with the evidence. Why does he not say '*present* faith in Christ?' The testimony is that his hope of salvation for some beyond the grave, was connected with the offer of Christ there. His statements, therefore, are not contradictory of the evidence. Nay, they confirm it. For this very soul upon which he says he would shut every door to which he had access but that of faith in Christ, he declares he would follow into the eternal world with "hopes," even if he saw the sinner die with "no evidence of repentance"! This is enough. It settles the case. Mr. Parker could not follow an impenitent soul into eternity with hope unless "he inclined to the belief" that there was hope for it there! And this is a soul, let it be observed, to whom Mr. P. is ministering. The explanation of the members of the Council, that the reference was to one who had never heard of Christ, is, in itself, a contradiction. He was one to whom Mr. Parker was actually preaching Christ. He was one whom he was supposed to meet in the actual discharge of his pastoral duties. It was a practical question of practical life. But the evidence does not rest upon this question. There is, as Dr. Vermilye has said, a mass of testimony quite distinct from this which stands unrefuted. It is a very significant thing, to which the defence does not even allude, that Mr. P's views had such hold upon his mind that they had found their way *into his written creed,* and that he *undertook to explain the articles of the church* in accordance with them. A defence in the face of such facts is either mere trifling or sheer desperation.

Now the question arises, Is a person in the state of mind in which Mr. Parker was, on the eleventh day of January, 1860, to be regarded as a qualified teacher of an orthodox Congregational Church? In examining this question, we must notice one or two views that have been presented.

Prof. Harris says (*Bost. Rec. March 1st.*) "The simple question," in such examination of a candidate, "is, are his christian belief and christian character such that he is worthy to be ordained as a minister of Christ?" According to this principle, a Congregational Council is bound to settle over a Congregational Church any Methodist, Baptist, Presbyterian, or Episcopalian who may apply, if "his christian belief and christian character are such that he is worthy to be ordained as a minister of Christ!" The implication here is that Congregationalism has no distinctive principles whatever. This is certainly liberal; but it is a liberality that will work the ruin of any organization adopting it.

Much stress has been laid upon the fact that Mr. Parker had *not* a definite faith upon certain points, as for example, the Trinity, and a future state of probation. Because he was not prepared absolutely to *reject* the tri-personality of the Godhead; because he did not *positively believe* that the impenitent dead would have a chance of salvation beyond the grave, his orthodoxy, it is argued, is not to be called in question.

Now this is the very point. Is a man to be regarded as sound in the faith who is not settled upon these points? Is he qualified for the ministry of an evangelical church if he has not a *definite faith* upon all the great fundamental truths of the gospel? How preposterous is it for a man to teach others to "continue in the faith, grounded and settled," who is himself all unsettled! We care not what a man's talents or personal character may be, if Christ has not taught him the great substantial truths of His gospel, He has not yet called him to preach that gospel; and no man has a right to ask entrance to the ministry of reconciliation, and no Council has a right to grant such entrance, unless the promise of Christ has been fulfilled, and the Holy Spirit has been given to lead the man into all essential truth. This we regard as a primary principle in the gospel ministry. It can never be rejected or neglected without peril.

Where these qualifications are wanting, the least that any man who desires the ministry can do, is to wait until they are obtained;

and the least that any Council can do, in such a case, is to require the man to wait; rather than by endorsing his errors and confirming him in them, inflict upon him, as well as upon the cause of truth and of Christ, a great and lasting injury.

Mr. Parker was endorsed by one of the most respectable Councils of New England; and he was endorsed, not with one or two diversities from the evangelical faith, but with the whole series presented before. It is clear, then, that in the judgment of this Council, neither one nor all these views combined, now constitute a bar to good and regular standing in the Congregational ministry. Nor does this case stand alone. It appears from the facts brought out in this controversy, that men may deny the plenary inspiration of the Scriptures, boldly affirming that parts of the Bible are not inspired; may be all unsettled as to the doctrine of eternal punishment; may, in Universalist pulpits, recognize the Christian character and standing of Universalism; may deny the doctrine of original sin; may affirm the sinner's ability to do all that God requires of him independent of Christ or of the Holy Spirit; may do all this without prejudicing their claim to ordination or to a full position in the Christian ministry. These are startling facts. The churches cannot safely sleep under them much longer.*

Yet it is not easy for many good men among us to believe that there is any serious peril. They are told that there is no change; that the same doctrines are taught now that have been held from the first; that the cry of danger is a vain alarm. Dr. Hawes, for example, in his last reconciliation with Dr. Bushnell, (*Religious Herald, June 1st*, 1854,) says, "I remain in the faith in which I entered the ministry; *in the faith in which the church was planted, which it has been my privilege to serve now thirty-six years; and which is held by the great body of evangelical churches and ministers in New England.*" Dr. Hawes thus claims for himself, and for those who agree with him, the original faith of the New England churches. And this is the claim, made everywhere so confidently and freely, that has secured general belief, and acquiesence in the present state of things in the churches. Efforts to effect a change for the

---

* It is worthy of notice that a short time previous to the ordination of Mr. Parker, Dr. Hawes himself had publicly expressed great anxiety in reference to the state of the Congregational churches. At a meeting of the Congregational Board of Publication in Boston he preached a sermon, a brief report of which was published. We cannot now lay our hand upon the report, but we recollect distinctly some of its points. Congregationalism, he maintained, had two great wants, a *common creed* and a *better organization*. We have, he said, no common standards and no common bond of unity. To the question, 'what is Congregationalism,' we cannot give an answer. *There are great divergencies in faith and practice among us.* Independency has no foundation in reason or scripture—in nature or grace. We must have a change, he urged, or we shall loose our hold on the conservative and thoughtful, and fall into the hands of the rash and the radical. These were Dr. Hawes' sentiments then. We can hardly understand how, within less than a year from that time, he could ridicule Mr. Childs' expressions of anxiety upon the same subject as "dolorously soloistic."

better have been met by the cry of "Presbyterianism—Princetonism—Triangular Theology," &c., and those who have seriously believed that there was a drifting away from the old foundations, and have endeavored earnestly and conscientiously to prevent it, have been held up as hostile to New England and her theology.

Now it is this claim that we propose to examine briefly in the light of the present controversy; and in doing so we shall be directly on the line of our main inquiry—the action of the Council in ordaining Mr. Parker over an orthodox Congregational church.

The first question is, What *is* the true New England theology? The second is, What doctrines are now held, and what were endorsed by the Hartford Council?

Fortunately we have no difficulty in determining the first of these questions. The original theology of New England is settled. It was declared again and again by solemn synodical action; and was confirmed by the preaching of the whole body of ministers to whom, under God, New England owes so much.

The synod which formed the Cambridge Platform met in 1648; the ministers and churches of Connecticut taking part in its action. This synod *unanimously* adopted the "*Westminster Confession of Faith*," as expressing the doctrinal belief of the ministers and churches of New England. This is the present standard of the Presbyterian Church. In 1680, a second synod in Boston adopted the *Savoy Confession*, which, in articles of faith, is almost identical with the Westminster Confession. The synod "in fact adopted both Confessions in one." "After the example of the synod of 1680, the churches and ministers of Connecticut, in 1708, met in a consociated Council and gave their consent to the Westminster and Savoy Confessions both. . . . . After the adoption of the Saybrook Platform, 'the ministers of Connecticut, in their public Conventions, several times renewed their consent to this Confession of Faith,' *which remains as it was when it first received their approbation, and as it was when it was approved by the New England Churches.*"[*]

The "Congregational Order" containing the standards of the Congregational Churches of Connecticut, was issued by order of the General Association of Connecticut as late as 1841; and approved by the General Association of Massachusetts the same year. We shall make this the basis of our examination. It is of course perfectly proper to test the faith of ministers and churches by their own standards.

I. In regard to *Inspiration*. The Congregational Confession after enumerating the books of the Bible, says, "*all* which are given by inspiration of God, to be the rule of faith and life."[†] And again, "The Old Testament in Hebrew, ... and the New Tes-

---

[*] Congregational order: Hist. account, &c., p. 16.   [†] Chap. 1, Sec. 2.

tament in Greek, ... being *immediately inspired* by God," &c.*
The New England fathers never thought of doubting the perfect plenary inspiration of Scripture. They held with Robinson, the father of their churches, that "the Scriptures have the Spirit of God for the author both of *matter and manner and writing.*"† They believed that what inspired men wrote, they wrote, "not in THE WORDS which man's wisdom teacheth, but which the Holy Ghost teacheth." I. Cor. 2: 13.

This verbal inspiration Mr. Parker emphatically rejected, and in his rejection was sustained by the Council. Nor would it seem now to be an uncommon case for candidates to be licensed and ordained, who openly declare that parts of the Bible are not inspired.

II. The teaching of the Congregational Confession in regard to the *Trinity* has been quoted in Mr. Childs' letter. (p. 15.)

III. Upon the subject of *Sin*, we give the whole chapter of the Confession; omitting the scripture proofs, for which we would refer our readers to the volume itself. (*pp.* 180–182.)

Confession of Faith, Chapter VI.

"Of the Fall of Man; of Sin; and of the Punishment thereof."

I. "God having made a covenant of works and life thereupon, with our first parents, and all their posterity in them, they being seduced by the subtilty and temptation of Satan, did wilfully transgress the law of their creation, and break the covenant in eating the forbidden fruit.

II. By this sin they, and we in them, fell from original righteousness and communion with God, and so became dead in sin, and wholly defiled in all the faculties and parts of soul and body.

III. They being the root, and by God's appointment standing in the room and stead, of all mankind, *the guilt of this sin was imputed, and corrupted nature conveyed, to all their posterity* descending from them by ordinary generation.

IV. From this original corruption whereby we are *utterly indisposed, disabled, and made opposite to all good,* and wholly inclined to all evil, do proceed all actual transgressions.

V. This corruption of nature during this life, doth remain in those that are regenerated; and although it be through Christ pardoned and mortified, yet *both itself and all the motions thereof are truly and properly sin.*

VI. Every sin, both *original* and actual, being a transgression of the righteous law of God, and contrary thereunto, doth *in its own nature, bring guilt upon the sinner, whereby he is bound over to the wrath of God, and curse of the law,* and so made subject to death, with all miseries, spiritual, temporal, and eternal."

These are the professed doctrines of the Congregational churches. Compare now with these the doctrines avowed by Mr. Parker and endorsed by the Hartford Council. "He declined to predicate sin of the nature of man." "I do not believe," says Mr. Parker, "that man is blameworthy either for his nature, or its hereditary corruption." (*Creed.*) This is a distinct rejection of the doctrine of orig-

---

* Chap. 1, Sec. 8.   † Works. Vol. 1, pp. 44–5.

inal sin. In this rejection Drs. Hawes and Spring heartily unite.
"Who does believe so?" they say, "or who can believe otherwise
than this article (of Mr. P.) expresses?" If they really wish to
know, we tell them that the whole evangelical church of God 'can
believe otherwise'; that all the fathers of the New England churches
did believe otherwise; that their own *Confession of Faith* teaches
otherwise; and—if we may come down to a more limited sphere
—that the whole line of pastors of the First Church of Hartford
down to the days of Dr. Hawes *have* believed otherwise.

The *Confession of Faith* of the Connecticut churches says, in regard to the original corruption of nature, "*Both itself and all the
motions thereof* ARE TRULY AND PROPERLY SIN;" and "every sin,
both *original* and actual .... doth in its own nature bring
guilt upon the sinner, *whereby he is bound over to the wrath of God
and curse of the law,* and so made subject to death with all miseries,
spiritual, temporal and eternal."

We presume we shall not be contradicted in saying that Dr.
Hawes is the first of the honored line of pastors of the First Church
of Hartford, who has rejected the great and fundamental doctrine
of *Original Sin!* Thomas Hooker was the first of those pastors.
Dr. Nathan Strong was the last, preceding Dr. Hawes.*

To give the full testimony of these men to this doctrine would
require a volume rather than a pamphlet page. Take the following
as a specimen of the teachings of the venerated Hooker. To the
sinner whom he would direct to Christ, he says, "Say—O Lord, I
have a CURSED NATURE; and though there were no devil, no world,
no temptations outwardly, yet this *cursed nature* of mine would sin
against thee." "Dost thou say it is *thy nature to sin?* Then I say,
the greater is thy wickedness; .... Therefore rather mourn
the more for thy sins, *because it is thy cursed nature so to do.*" ("Soul's
Preparation for Christ." pp. 40–41.)

The writings of Dr. Strong are burdened with the deep and
awful and *sinful* depravity of human nature. "Both experience
and Scripture testimony," he says, "afford abundant conviction that
*every creature of the human race, is, from the beginning, possessed of a
nature corrupt and* GUILTY." (Sermon at the ordination of Joseph
Strong.) "The need of regeneration implies the *natural and total
wickedness of the heart.*" (Sermons, vol. 2, p. 158.)

---

*Mr. Hooker was one of the ablest of the New England ministers. The estimation
in which he was held in the Reformed Church, may be judged from the fact that he
was invited to sit as a member of the Westminster Assembly. His church at Hartford was the first in Connecticut; and "embraced the territory now occupied by the
churches of the city; of East Hartford and of West Hartford." This fact is of interest
as showing "the Faith in which" all "these churches were planted."

Dr. Strong was one of the leading ministers of New England at the close of the
last century and the commencement of the present. The relation of the First Church
of Hartford, therefore, to the other churches of Connecticut, and especially to those
represented in the Council which ordained Mr. Parker, justifies our special reference
to its original faith.

All men, he affirms, "*come into the world with sinful hearts,*" and "when the Scriptures speak of any exercises in the human heart that are pleasing to God, they ascribe them to an origin perfectly consistent with the doctrine of a *total moral corruption of human nature.*" (Sermon on Depravity.)

Dr. Hawes maintains that "a child, properly speaking, has no character." "Character," he says, "is not anything which is born with us or makes an essential, constituent part of us. It is not inherited by birth, nor transmitted by natural descent from parent to child." (Sermon on Character, &c., pp. 6, 8.)

Dr. Strong says, "The *natural, unholy* CHARACTER of man is an *essential* truth to be *plainly taught by Christian ministers.*" "If this doctrine be false," he maintains, "the whole gospel is false; and in the same proportion as men believe the reality, the extensiveness and the *guiltiness* of our *natural character* in the sight of God, they will see the need of a gospel," &c.* Dr. Hawes denies the naturally sinful character of men. Dr. Strong maintains that such denial involves the denial of the whole gospel. And yet Dr. Hawes says he "remains in the faith in which his church was planted!"

IV. In regard to the doctrine of *Ability*, Drs. Hawes and Spring say:

"As to what the letter charges, that the candidate holds that every man has ability, in the sense of 'adequate power,' to fulfill the commands of God—let that speak for itself. It is accounted no deadly heresy, at least in this part of the country, to hold that man has power to do what God commands him to do ; or that he cannot be justly blamed or punished for not doing impossibilities ;" (p. 9—note).

This is the plain, unambiguous statement of the doctrine of plenary ability. It is not even shaded by the distinction of "natural" and "moral ability."†

---

* Sermons at the ordinations of J. Strong and of J. L. Skinner.

† It is well known that since the days of Edwards, many have used the term "natural ability," as he did, to denote simply *moral agency*, without intending at all to deny the sinner's real and utter inability to the great end of his own salvation, or his absolute dependence on the Holy Spirit for every saving grace. It is equally well known that others—of late especially—have taken advantage of this, to foist in and establish the doctrine of the sinner's full and complete ability in himself to meet all the requirements of God ; and that they have claimed for this doctrine the support of men, living and dead, by whom their views have ever been held in abhorrence. The late venerable Dr. Tyler suffered much from this source. Adopting the common phraseology of "natural ability," (by which he affirmed, however, he "meant nothing more than the possession of those faculties which are essential to moral agency,") he was claimed as an ally by men and schools whose principles he utterly repudiated. His name was employed to sanction doctrines which his soul loathed. It was in view of this, as we understand it, that he remarked at the close of his life, "that, inasmuch as some terms used by him many years ago, were now liable to be misunderstood, and their meaning perverted, he should substitute other terms for them, or be more cautious in using them without careful explanation." (Memoir, p. 108.)

May it not be wise for us to receive the suggestion of this venerated man ? Inasmuch as the term "natural ability" *is* "misunderstood and its meaning perverted "— inasmuch as moral ability is really the only ability that comes into the question—inas-

It is the assertion, as clear as words can make it, that it is no heresy here to hold that the sinner has full power to make himself a new heart; to repent; to believe in Christ; to be holy as God is holy. For all these things "God commands him to do." This teaching is, of course, in direct contradiction to the word of God. "A new heart will I GIVE YOU;" "Christ has been exalted to GIVE repentance;" "Faith is the GIFT of God;" are passages which, with hundreds more of the same nature, the Evangelical Church has ever been wont to regard as indicating the absolute dependence of men upon the sovereign grace of God for these gifts. Of course there can be no such dependence if every man "has power to do all that God commands him to do." We are then driven to the ground that has been openly taken among us, that there is no absolute necessity of the Holy Spirit to renew and save the soul!

God commands all men to come to Christ. If God commands it, Drs. Hawes and Spring say they can do it. Against this assertion we must receive the equally positive one of Christ himself: "No man CAN come to me, except the Father which hath sent me draw him." (John 6: 44.)

The doctrine of ability is also in express contradiction of the standards of Congregationalism.

The *Confession of Faith* (chap. 9, sec. 3,) says:

"Man by his fall into a state of sin, hath *wholly lost all ability of will to any spiritual good* accompanying salvation, so as a natural man, being altogether averse from that good, and dead in sin, *is not able by his own strength* to convert himself, or to *prepare himself* thereunto."

And again: (chap. 16, sec. 3,)

"Their (believers') ability to do good works is *not at all of themselves, but wholly from the Spirit of Christ.*"

See also chap. 6, sec. 4, already quoted, p. 51.

Thomas Hooker, in a discourse upon Luke 1: 17, proposes to establish, among others, the following points:—"That a man must *will* to receive Christ and grace before he can receive them. That no man of himself, voluntarily, *can will* that he may receive Christ. Lastly, that *God will work a will* in his servants to receive the Lord Jesus Christ."

God commands all men everywhere to repent. According to the doctrine endorsed by Drs. Hawes and Spring, if God commands it, it is in their own power. Hooker says, "If thou didst consider

---

much as "natural ability," after all, leaves the sinner at an infinite remove from the end in view, namely, his regeneration and salvation, and therefore is not in any proper sense an *ability* to this end—inasmuch as "moral agency" can be maintained in perfect consistency with the sinner's true inability and his absolute dependence on Divine grace—inasmuch as, by persisting in the use of the term, we are now obviously and strongly playing into the hands of errorists, may it not be wise and right to lay it aside and unite with the great body of the Church of Christ in all ages, in affirming simply the sinner's *inability* "to any spiritual good accompanying salvation."

thy own weakness thou wouldst not say that repentance is in thine own power. Remember what the apostle says: If peradventure God would *give* repentance, &c."*

God requires of sinners a change of heart. This also must of course be in their own power if they can do all that God requires. Dr. Strong contends that "men *cannot* change their own hearts:" "Sinners," he says "may imagine they can turn when they please; but they will never *please* to turn until they are *turned by Almighty power;*" and he adds: "I do not see how those who deny the need of a new heart, or the *necessity* of the Holy Spirit to *give* this heart, can afterwards come forward and call themselves sound believers in Christ or of the Scripture."†

If it be said that those who hold the doctrine of ability do not deny the necessity of the Spirit, we ask how that can be? If the sinner has in himself "adequate power" to fulfil the commands of God, what possible necessity can there be for any more power? If he can do all that God requires of him, it is enough; he needs no Holy Spirit. This is the necessary, logical issue of the doctrine of the sinner's ability. It destroys the whole system of grace. If that system is to stand, this doctrine must be modified so as really to mean 'no ability,' or it must be given up. For ourselves, we choose to unite in the confession of Inspiration and of the Evangelical Church, and say, "We are not sufficient of ourselves to think any-thing, as of ourselves; but our sufficiency is of God." (2 Cor. 3:5.)

To say that a sinner has any real ability or *adequate power* to do all that God requires of him, is contradictory not only to the Scriptures and the universal faith of the Church, but to all true Christian experience. God requires us to be holy as He is holy. Every true Christian knows that he is not holy, and he knows that he cannot make himself holy. He knows that nothing but Almighty power and grace can make him holy. To tell him otherwise, is to contradict the deepest convictions of his Christian consciousness and the teachings of the Spirit of God within him.

V. In reference to the salvation of the heathen, we quote simply this article of the Confession. (Chap. 10, sec. 4.)

" Others not elected, although they may be called by the ministry of the word, and may have some common operations of the Spirit, yet not being effectually drawn by the Father, they neither do nor can come unto Christ, and therefore can not be saved ; *much less can men not professing the Christian religion, be saved in any other way whatso-ever, be they never so diligent to frame their lives according to the light of nature, and the law of that religion they do profess ; and to assert and maintain that they may, is very per-nicious, and to be detested.*"

If any intelligent man chooses seriously to say that this is the

---

*Soul fitted for Christ, p. 50.
† Sermon at ordination of J. L. Skinner ; and Sermons, vol. 1, p. 262.

same doctrine that was promulged by Mr. Parker on his ordination, and has since been taught from his pulpit, it is hardly worth while to argue the point. Argument would go very little ways with one who could see no difference between the above article, and the doctrine that a heathen, the last act of whose life was one of gross idolatry, 'undoubtedly went to heaven!'

VI. Touching the *design of Christ's death*, the Congregational Confession says:

"As God hath appointed the elect unto glory, so hath he by the eternal and most free purpose of his will fore-ordained all the means thereunto. Wherefore they *who are elected*, being fallen in Adam, *are redeemed by Christ*, are effectually called unto faith in Christ by his Spirit working in due season, are justified, adopted, sanctified, and kept by his power through faith unto salvation. *Neither are any other redeemed by Christ*, or effectually called, justified, adopted, sanctified, and saved, *but the elect only.*" (Chap. 3, sec. 6.)

Robinson, the father of New England Congregationalism, says: "Christ died effectually and in his and his Father's *intention* of love, for them *only* that are saved." (Works, v. 1, pp. 333, 334.)

"Do you think, brethren," says Thomas Shepard, one of the greatest and holiest of the New England fathers; "Do you think that Christ's blood was shed to work no more in his people than in hypocrites? . . . If Christ should have died as much for Judas as for Peter, . . then Peter had no more cause of blessing Christ for his love in redeeming him than Judas!" (Works, v. 2, pp. 208, 209.)

"Christ," says Hooker, "will not miss his end; he came for the lost *sheep;* then the lost sheep he will have; and though the lost sheep can not seek nor save themselves, yet Christ will save them."

"Christ never prayed for the world, and he will never save the world." (Soul's Prep. for Christ, pp. 39, 159.)

When Christ shall appear with all his ransomed church before the Father in glory, Edwards represents him as saying, "Here am I, and the children which thou hast given me;" "as much as to say," Edwards adds, "Here am I, with every one of those whom thou gavest me from eternity to take care of, that they might be redeemed and glorified; and *to redeem* WHOM, I have done and suffered so much," &c. (Works v. 1, p. 504.)

"Christ," says Dr. Strong, "has suffered and become a ransom for all *those who are his.*" (Sermons, v. 1, p. 131.)

This was the doctrine of all the New England fathers, and of the New England churches. It was the faith in which the First Church of Hartford was "planted." The founders of that Church with the whole body of their co-laborers in New England, believed that God will accomplish all he undertakes. They believed that if God eternally *designed* that the death of His Son should have the same relation to, and effect upon, all men, it will have the same. If Christ died with the same design to save all men, all will be saved.

They believed it to be a denial of the character of God, and the destruction of the hopes of the Church, to say that Christ, in his death, had just as much *intention* to save Judas Iscariot as the Apostle Paul. This is not a question as to the *sufficiency* or *value* of the atonement, which all admit to be infinite; but as to the eternal *purpose* of the Father as executed in the mission of the Son. Robinson only uttered the voice of Evangelical Christendom when he said—"They for whom Christ died never perish." To deny this "impeacheth God's power, and makes him unable (do what he can) to save any more than he doth save, though he desire it never so much." (Works, v. 1, pp. 333, 334.) The Church has always understood Christ to have meant something when he said— "I lay down my life *for the sheep*." It is not our purpose now, however, to argue this point. We are simply stating the doctrine of the New England standards and the New England fathers.— That they held, with one accord, to the doctrine of a definite atonement, is just as clear as that they held to any atonement.

VII. Upon the *Future State*, it will be sufficient to quote the explicit language of the Confession. Until recently there has been no diversity of sentiment upon this subject among those who claim to be orthodox Congregationalists.

The Confession (chap. 31, sec. 1) says:

" The bodies of men after death return to dust, and see corruption, but their souls, (which neither die nor sleep,) having an immortal subsistence, immediately return to God who gave them; the souls of the righteous being then made perfect in holiness, are received into the highest heavens where they behold the face of God in light and glory, waiting for the full redemption of their bodies ; and the souls of the wicked are cast into hell, where they remain in torment, and utter darkness, reserved for the judgment of the great day ; *besides these two places of souls separated from their bodies, the Scriptures acknowledgeth none.*"

It is clear, then, that upon all these points the New England churches have a well defined and positive faith. These standards have never been formally renounced. Nay, it is claimed that they have not been departed from. It is perfectly fair, therefore, to test the faith of the ministry by these standards. It is unfair for any man to reject the doctrines of these standards and still say that he holds the faith in which the New England churches were planted. Against this we protest. If a man chooses to deny these doctrines, he is at liberty to do so; if he has any which he thinks better, it is a wonder that he does not wish to proclaim them; but to renounce the old faith and to teach doctrines subversive of it, and still profess before the people to cling to it, is what we can not reconcile with good faith.

Judged by these standards, it is plain that the doctrines avowed and endorsed at Hartford, are very wide departures from the true faith of the New England churches. If that faith is scriptural and safe, this is unscriptural and perilous.

These facts show, too, how uncandid it was for Drs. Hawes and Spring to dismiss the points in controversy, with one exception, as unessential, or as constituting the debated ground between Presbyterians and Congregationalists. If the points were unimportant at last, they were so at first; and their strong denials and denunciations were uncalled for. If they were sufficiently important at first to demand their earnest defence, they are important still, and these gentlemen are not at liberty thus to dismiss them.

Nor do these points constitute the debatable ground between Presbyterians and Congregationalists as such. The *Confession of Faith* shows conclusively that the doctrines which Mr. Parker denied, and whose denial the Council endorsed, are a part of the professed faith of the Congregational churches of Connecticut. They are a substantial part of the faith in which the churches of New England were founded. If they are now disputed ground it can only be because some among us have departed from that faith. Let them depart if it must be so, but let them not denounce and revile those who prefer to abide in the faith in which our fathers lived and died.*

---

*It does seem to us time we were done with the miserable attempts to forestall the defence of truth and the exposure of error, by the perpetual cry of "Presbyterianism." The simple fact is, the *professed* doctrines of Congregationalism and Presbyterianism are identical. The doctrines now held and taught in the Old School Presbyterian Church are neither more nor less than the precise doctrines of the New England standards and the New England fathers. To denounce and ridicule these doctrines is to denounce and ridicule the original faith of New England. To overthrow these is to overthrow the foundations of the New England churches. Let us understand then what those men are doing who appeal to the churches by the outcry of "Presbyterianism" and "Princetonism." Let us understand that under this cover the battle is waged against the bulwarks of our faith—against the foundations of the true New England theology and of the word of God.

It deserves to be said that our fathers had none of this jealousy of Presbyterianism. They were neither afraid nor ashamed of the name. The writer has before him two volumes of "Sermons by Nathan Strong; Pastor of the North PRESBYTERIAN Church, in Hartford, Conn.," printed in 1798-1800. Dr. Strong, as we have said, was the immediate predecessor of Dr. Hawes. In 1799 the *Hartford North Association* of Ministers, composed of such men as Drs. Strong and Flint of Hartford, and Dr. Perkins of West Hartford, made the following declaration of their principles :—

" This Association give information to all whom it may concern, that the constitution of the churches in the State of Connecticut, founded on the common usages, and the Confession of Faith, Heads of Agreement, and articles of Church Discipline, adopted at the earliest period of the settlement of the State, *is not Congregational, but contains the essentials of the government of the Church of Scotland, or [the] Presbyterian Church in America ;* particularly as it gives a decisive power to ecclesiastical councils ; and a consociation, consisting of ministers and messengers. or a lay representation from the churches, is possessed of substantially the same authority as Presbytery. The judgments, decisions, and censures in our churches and in the Presbyterian are mutually deemed valid. *The churches therefore, in Connecticut at large, and in our district in particular, are not now, and never were, from the earliest period of our settlement Congregational churches,* according to the ideas and forms of church order contained in the Book of Discipline. called the Cambridge Platform. There are, however, scattered over the State, perhaps ten or twelve churches (*unconsociated*) which are properly called Congregational, agreeably to the rules of Church Discipline, in the book above mentioned. Sometimes indeed, the associated churches of Connecticut are loosely and vaguely, though improperly termed Congregational. While our churches in the State at large are, in the most essential and important respects, the same as the Presbyterian, still in minute and unimportant points of church order and discipline, both we and the Presbyterian Church in America acknowledge a difference."

According to this testimony the true and proper form of the Connecticut churches is *Presbyterian*, and not Congregational. And can any man doubt where Drs. Strong and Perkins would have stood at such a time as this ? Would they have opposed sound Presbyterianism for the sake of unsound Congregationalism ?

We submit these pages to our brethren in the churches and ministry of New England. We only ask for them a candid consideration. We have written as we have solemnly believed the truth and the highest interests of the church demanded. If the fears expressed shall prove unfounded, no man will rejoice more than the writer. But let us not forget that apostasy from the faith always comes in gradually. Here is our peril. "Giving up one truth," says Dr. Strong, "is only preparing the way to give up another." The whole history of the Church proves it. Every great and fatal defection from the faith follows this law. First one truth is given up, then another, and another, until shipwreck has been made of the whole Christian system. Can we claim exemption from this law? Is it sure, because we have the Puritan for our father, that we can never be given up to the rejection of the Puritan faith? Glance back for a few years. Does any man believe that fifty years ago the ordination of a man holding such views as Mr. Parker's could have taken place in the city of Hartford? Would Dr. Hawes have been ordained avowing such sentiments? Could a Council have been found who would have hesitated for an instant to refuse ordination in such a case? This is a great change to take place in a single generation. And now what is the prospect for the future? When Drs. Hawes and Spring are in their graves, and such men as these whom they are now placing over other churches, are gathered to ordain *their* successors, what manner of ordination shall it be? Whom would these men not ordain? Whom would they reject? We put the case solemnly to these venerable fathers. Their work must soon close. Surely it is something to them what is to be the destiny of the churches they leave behind them.

Dr. Hawes closes his letter of reconciliation to Dr. Bushnell in these words: "Sure I am that my sun will go down brighter, and I shall leave this much loved field of my labors and my prayers with a happier mind and more cheerful hopes, if, as I close my course, I may think of these dear churches of our Lord as rooted and grounded in the truth, and their pastors as happily united in fellowship and love, and contending earnestly for the faith once delivered to the saints." (*Religious Herald*, June 1, 1854.)

By all the force of this impressive declaration, we appeal to this venerable man to lend his influence for the brief remnant of his days, to secure the issue he so earnestly desires, by securing for the churches *pastors* "rooted and grounded in the truth," and willing to "contend earnestly for the faith once delivered to the saints."

Here we dismiss the subject. We have no desire for controversy for its own sake. We would not needlessly offend one of our brethren in Christ. New England is dear to us, and will be while we live. Here are the homes and the graves of our fathers; and here, if God will, we wait our own charge. We protest against the unjust clamor that we are hostile to New England and her faith. We yield to no man in all due love to the land of our birth. We believe most firmly and heartily in her glorious old faith. We believe it to be "the faith of God's elect;" and because we believe so ; and because we believe that faith is in peril ; because we believe the future welfare and glory of New England are wrapped in it; because we believe her woe and shame lie in its rejection, we plead for its deliverance.

And that deliverance, we are fully assured, will come. If it tarry we will wait for it; but that it will come, sooner or later, we have no more doubt than we have that the glory of the Lord shall cover the earth. This is the strong consolation of those who, now, amidst opposition and reproach, contend for the faith delivered to the saints. Error may triumph for a time ; but in its own nature, and in the fulfilment of God's glorious promises to the Church, it must perish. The word of the Lord abideth forever.

THE MANCHESTER CASE.

THE ORDINATION OF MR. DORMAN.*

After the substance of the preceding pages had been prepared, an event occurred which casts important light upon the facts of the above case.

On the 31st of May, 1860, a Council was called to ordain and install Mr. L. M. Dorman as pastor of the Congregational Church in Manchester, Ct. Mr. Dorman had been licensed to preach by the Third (New School) Presbytery of New York, about two years before. It deserves to be said, however, that at his ordination he refused to give his assent, in part at least, to the Confession of Faith of the Presbyterian Church.

"The following ministers were present at the Council, with four or five delegates: Rev. Dr. Calhoun, of Coventry ; Rev. Messrs. Cheeseboro, of Glastenbury ; Snow, of Eastbury ; L. Hyde, of Vernon ; S. B. Forbes and H. Day of North Manchester. . . . The body, though small, embraced representatives of the two schools of New England Theology.

---

* The facts in regard to this case are derived from the Hartford *Daily Times* and the *Boston Recorder.* The article in the former was evidently written by some one friendly to Mr. Dorman. The articles of the *Recorder* appeared, one (July 12,) over the signature " H. R. ;" the other, (Aug. 9,) signed by Rev. G. A. Oviatt, Scribe of the Council which settled Mr. Dorman. The correctness of the statements has not been called in question.

The examination proved unsatisfactory. The lax views of the candidate on inspiration, election, depravity, and above all, probation after death, rendered it impossible for the Council to proceed. In this judgment they were unanimous." The result is thus stated in the *Hartford Times*, of June 2d :

"The Congregational Society in Manchester is quite excited over the action of the Ecclesiastical Council which met in that place on Thursday, to ordain the new pastor chosen by the Society, the Rev. Mr. Dorman. Although the Society (a large and important one,) are unanimous for Mr. Dorman, yet the Council refused to ordain him. The alleged reason was, that in his examination they had obliged him, by close questioning, to admit that he was not clear in his own mind on certain doctrinal points. These points (which, we believe, relate to certain accepted but abstruse and little-understood notions concerning the exact nature of the Trinity, &c.,) are not considered by Mr. D.'s friends as being in any sense vital, or affecting in any degree his standing as an orthodox believer in the essential points of the New England creed. They are precisely the same on which Dr. Vermilye and other disciples of the rigid old East Windsor school of theology opposed the ordination of the Rev. Mr. Parker, of the Hartford South Church, last January; and it is maintained by Mr. Dorman's friends that the delegates who composed the Council, were influenced in their unexpected action, by a reluctance to override Dr. Vermilye's precedent on that occasion. It was not a full Council; and the Society, as soon as the decision was announced, at once gave notice of *another meeting* on Monday, to call another Council. They expect the second Council will act in a less arbitrary and illiberal spirit, and ordain the minister they want. If not, they are determined to have him at any rate, and will take measures to accomplish their object without the agency of the Council."

A second Council was called, and met on the 6th of June—within less than a week from the adjournment of the first. This "Council consisted of Dr. Hawes, and Rev. Messrs. Parker, Webber, and Burton of Hartford, and Dr. Spring of East Hartford, and Rev. Messrs. Cheeseboro of Glastenbury, Oviatt of Somers, Fessenden of Ellington, Clapp of Rockville, and Forbes of North Manchester, with delegates sufficient to make the whole number in attendance twenty." Dr. Hawes was chosen moderator, and took the leading part in the examination. A correspondent of the *Recorder* (H. R.) thus reports:

"The Moderator and his associates were not a little troubled to ascertain what Mr. Dorman believed on some important points, and some of them were still more troubled by his explicit avowals on other points.

On the question whether the Gospel will be offered to any of the human race in the future world who die impenitent, the candidate was more reserved than when before the first Council, but there was no retraction or essential modification of the views then expressed. He admitted no connection between Adam's sin and the sin and ruin of his posterity except what he was pleased to state thus:—"Adam set a very bad example." The Bible was written only in part by inspiration of God. By *election* we are to understand simply, that God foresaw who would accept the Gospel, and them he determined to save. He thought it probable, and after much questioning he was almost confident, that all true believers will persevere in holiness and be finally saved. On the doctrine of divine decrees the answers were so singular that Dr. Hawes referred the candidate to his license, which certified his assent to the creed of the Presbyterian Church. But he declined giving his assent, at Manchester, to the doctrine in question as laid down in the Presbyterian Confession of Faith. The Moderator then produced the creed of the church over which it was proposed to ordain him. He was understood to dissent positively from the Manchester Confession, also, respecting the decrees of God."

Rev. Mr. Oviatt, who was certainly not unfriendly to Mr. Dorman or the Council says:

"During the early part of the examination, Mr. Dorman appeared tolerably well; during the latter part, far otherwise. To many of the leading questions, his answers were very equivocal, certainly "non-committal." I remember distinctly the questions I put to him, and his answers thereto, almost word for word. I will give them in substance, and nearly verbatim, without the quotation marks. What is election?— Answer.—I suppose God's choosing some. Why does God choose some? Answer. I cannot tell. I sometimes lean to the opinion that God chooses some for reasons best known to himself, and sometimes I lean to the opinion that God chooses whom he does, because he foresees that they will repent and believe in Christ ; and therefore he elects them. I read the article in the "Confession of Faith" of the Church in Manchester, on election, and asked the candidate how he would expound it in a sermon, should his people request him to preach on this doctrine. Answer.—I don't know ; I am studying the Bible to find out. With regard to probation, I asked him, do you or do you not believe that the probation of all men ends at death?— Answer.—I cannot tell. God will give all men a fair chance. Faith in Christ is necessary to salvation. There may be some, I sometimes think, who, not having a sufficient knowledge of Christ in this world, will have an offer of pardon after death. I am not satisfied on this subject. About it I have my doubts. I don't know that any to whom I may ever preach in this land, will be among the number of those who have another chance after death. I asked, On what texts do you ground the belief of a probation *for any*, after death? Answer.—"All manner of sin and blasphemy shall be forgiven unto men; but the blasphemy against the Holy Ghost shall not be forgiven unto men." &c.

The license to preach, given to him by (I think) the Third Presbytery of New York, which specifies that he in his examination by that body assented to the "Confession of Faith," was read, when the Moderator asked him, Do you now believe as you did at the time this license was given to you? Answer.—I don't know but I do. Do you believe in the main, in the Assembly's Catechism? Answer.—I don't know. I don't know much about the Catechism. With regard to the "Perseverance of the Saints," the candidate was equivocal, undetermined in his answers. All through the examination, the candidate was, in respect to many leading, fundamental doctrines thus indefinite in his statements : seldom answering a question definitely, distinctly.

I was unwilling to ordain and install Mr. Dorman ; to me, the way was not open thus to proceed for these reasons :—1. I seriously thought Mr. Dorman unsound in *the faith*, in some essential particulars. 2. I thought he was too undetermined in his faith, was too full of doubts, leaned in too many different directions to be set over the church in Manchester."

The examination lasted from three to four hours, and resulted in a vote, by a majority of four, to proceed to the ordination. On this majority were Dr. Hawes, Dr. Spring, and Mr. Parker; the latter gentleman, having exerted himself earnestly to secure the result; and "on giving the right hand of fellowship, assured the pastor that he voted for him *most cordially.*" When the decision had been, reached, part of the Council withdrew, and the rest proceeded to the ordination.

The above we believe is a mild statement of the case. Mr. Oviatt's report, we have reason to suppose, was intended to be as favorable to Mr. Dorman and the Council as it could fairly be. He confines himself chiefly to that part of the examination which he himself conducted. No reply has been made to any of the reports.

In view of this case, it may be observed—

1. It abundantly confirms the statements made in regard to the Hartford ordination. Those who felt constrained to condemn the action of the Council in that case could ask no more complete justification than is furnished here.

2. It illustrates strikingly the point made in the preceding review, in regard to future danger, (p. 59). It answers, in part, the question, "Whom would these men not ordain?" Mr. Parker can work earnestly, and "vote *most cordially*" for the ordination of a man whom one Council has rejected unanimously, and in regard to whom the greater part even of the Council which ordained him, are "perplexed" and "dissatisfied." Is there no downward process here? One of the correspondents of the *Recorder* states, that at the examination of Mr. Dorman, "a member of the Manchester Church expressed his concern at finding that certain young preachers hold that salvation will be offered to some who die impenitent." "A theological student," with whom he was conversing, "*assured him that most of his associates in professional study adopted that opinion.*" The correspondent asks with point, "Is this one of the signs of the times?"

3. This case cannot be met by the cry of "Presbyterianism." The witnesses have not "looked from a Presbyterian stand-point." They are all Congregationalists; and so gross was the case that Congregationalists of both the Old and New Schools, had "no diversity of opinion touching the examination of Mr. Dorman." *Defenders of Dr. Bushnell could not vote for a man whom Drs. Hawes and Spring could ordain!*

4. Doctrinally the case was substantially like that at Hartford. This appears not only from the reports, but from the thorough endorsement of Mr. Dorman by Mr. Parker. It is hardly conceivable that Mr. Parker could have "voted most cordially" for Mr. Dorman, if he had not cordially sympathized with him. It throws, therefore, a decisive light upon the Hartford ordination. It settles Mr. Parker's position. It shows what such fathers of the Church as Drs. Hawes and Spring mean by "orthodoxy." To say that "the Bible is written only in part by inspiration"—to deny original sin—to be all unsettled in regard to election, the perseverance of the

saints, and the future state of those dying out of Christ—to be wholly indefinite and ignorant "in respect to many leading, *fundamental* doctrines"—to hold views in direct conflict with the Congregational Confession of Faith, and with the Articles of the church over which a man seeks ordination; all this, in the judgment of these venerable men, is not inconsistent with good standing in the orthodox Congregational ministry. This is an important point for the churches to understand. It is a point that is now settled beyond controversy. Its bearing upon the preceding discussion is obvious.

5. It is a remarkable case in ecclesiastical order. Here is a candidate who rejects not only the common standards of Congregationalism, but the particular Articles of the Church over which he is to be settled—a man so thoroughly unsound that a Council of Old and New School men *unanimously* refuse to ordain him: another Council is immediately called, and in the face of the former Council, proceed to the ordination! A regular Congregational Council declares a man unqualified for the Congregational ministry: within less than a week from that time, this man, by the action of another Congregational Council, is in full and regular standing in that ministry! Is this the legitimate working of the system? If so, we agree fully with Dr. Hawes, that "there must be a change, or we shall lose our hold upon the conservative and the thoughtful, and fall into the hands of the rash and the radical."